The Crystal Wing

by P.J. Chiuchiolo

The Crystal Wing

by P.J. Chiuchiolo

Railroad Street Press
394 Railroad Street, Suite 2
St. Johnsbury, VT 05819

Published in the United States by Railroad Street Press, St. Johnsbury, Vermont.

ISBN: 9781936711093

Library of Congress Control Number Pending
1.   Fiction

Jacket design by Susanna V. Walden.

First Print Edition 2011

Railroad Street Press
394 Railroad Street, Suite 2
St. Johnsbury, VT 05819
(802) 748-3551
www.railroadstreetpress.com

For You

Listen.

Listen with your heart.

Listen with your soul.

FIARA

1

The early morning mist hugged the still face of Lake Tazia, while a mild breeze gathered strength over its waters. The force of the wind rapidly brushed the water towards the land in ripples that rushed and pushed. A shiver of excitement moved through his stomach as he sensed the morning sun. The thick dampness of the air nestled along the water, like a cloud daring the light to shine.

He looked over his shoulder onto a length of beach, watching the shadow of his friend, John, disappear around a bend in the jagged shoreline. Lake Tazia, with its broad sprawling channels of water, teased him into the heart of Fiara. For miles it moved with diverse shoreline and dense forests. It was the gateway to the East and a hub for traffic into the North and the South. John and he had used its wooded arms for shelter and refuge. They received the abundance of its waters in fish and mollusks each time they journeyed across the land.

The sun broke through the morning mist, brilliantly reflecting against the water. He squinted and turned. A bird fluttered its wings, beating against the air as it made a landing in the damp sand. It arched its wings in graceful dance, punctuating the calm with a piercing cry. Watching the bird strut and coo, pecking at a still figure lying in the sand of the beach, he felt tense. He darted toward it, startling the bird into frenzy, but he didn't stop until he lifted the old man into his arms.

"Who are you?" the old man's pain scraped across his vocal cords.

"James. James McCautry."

At his answer, the old man touched the crystal wing hidden underneath the cloth of his breast pocket. He looked deeply into the young man's eyes and smiled.

"He won't even make it past Epping, let alone to the Sea of Abyss." John stirred the coals of the fire, sticking the ash in irritation.

"I think he'll make it if he has some help."

"I suppose you're going to take him."

James looked deeply into the glowing embers of the fire.

"I thought so. I've known you a long time. But, don't forget we play in Sumatra tomorrow night. After we're through, you can do as you like. Until then, I have a stake in this. They hired a duo. That's you and me."

They were hired to play for the Festival of Reanoke in the city of Sumatra. It took several years of hard work to accrue enough status to perform even at a small tavern in the heart of the city during the Festival. The Festival of Reanoke was the highlight of the musical season within the world of Fiara. Every musician fought for an opportunity to show talent there. James and John had spent their whole career vying for a chance to prove their gifts. There wasn't time to go to the sea.

The Sea of Abyss was an angry and violent body of water. It surrounded Fiara, terrorizing the people who had access to its waters. In the northeastern section of the world, the shore was open. Long ago, along the northern shore, the land split into cracks and crevasses that spew fire and molten rock. The southern shore, strewn with layers of stone called magnarus, seeped liquid that bubbled and rolled away from its surface spilling over like living fingers to form whirling pools. The pools churned rapidly against the shore. The hot liquid rivers and streams crisscrossed the surface of the shoreline, emptying into the waters of the sea. There, between the water and the land, a heavy steam trimmed the world. The fog rolled inland, bearing east, covering the land with a thick murky cloud hiding the entrance to the bogs and the mountains of the coast.

The bogs clung along the treacherous slopes of the mountain range called Pilchard. The entrance to the mountains was protected by a natural stone wall. It was called the Epping wall. The sharp angular slopes of the Pilchard Mountains ran uninterrupted for miles, dipping with drastic vertical drop into the Sea of Abyss. The Sea of Abyss surrounded the land of Fiara, except in the west.

The West had no shoreline. It emptied into light.

From the light, the Arca V'ing Enta rose. It covered the horizon as far as the eye could see, a bow of colored lights dancing across the sky. It sparkled day and night, tantalizing and teasing the imagination with wonder. No one knew what lay beyond it. No one could draw near enough to find out. They could only dream of what lie beyond, and from their dreams tell stories.

The Arca V'ing Enta brought dreams for the weary. The Sea of Abyss stormed the shore with fear.

James remembered sitting with the village men, a child, wide-eyed, listening to the vivid tales of the sea. He cringed as each word painted a darker picture and smothered him in its heavy blanket. In those fearful moments, he lifted his eyes to Neppam, an elder of the village. He found comfort in his gray bearded face, the wrinkles that marked his earnest countenance, the steady grinding of his sturdy jaw.

James looked intently at Tabum. Heavy breathing marked his struggle for life. He felt uneasy. Looking at Tabum, he was haunted by the memory of Neppam.

2

One evening, after the villagers had retired, Neppam and his servant Kalem moved into a small house on the outskirts of Poule. His abrupt appearance in the dead of night sparked rumors that stirred a whirlwind throughout the quiet climate of the village. Some people believed he was a sage. Some claimed he was a wizard seeking refuge in the tranquil countryside. With careful and astute precision, he blended into the local culture. His towering height and articulate stateliness enhanced the aura of mystery and intrigue surrounding him.

Neppam never spoke about his past. He walked the streets of Poule before the noonday sun touched its apex. In the afternoon, he joined the villagers in the square by the well. In the early morning, he bathed in the first light of dawn marking his walk into the Ansling Hills.

It was a crisp day, the dew wet and dripping over the warm colors of the fields. Neppam ignored the subtle stirring of morning sounds rolling across the brush and grass. His ears caught a melody, clear and soft, mingling within the distant noise from the village. He followed the melody through a cluster of trees to a small stream cutting into the edge of the field.

"It's beautiful," he whispered.

James scrambled to his feet. Brushing his clothes, he lowered his eyes.

"Where did you learn that song?"

"I made it up."

Neppam raised his eyebrows to the boy's words. He looked at the boy, then to the hills. "I've some food, if you're hungry."

Neppam smiled as he shared his food with the young boy. He watched him shove bread and cheese into his mouth. "What instrument do you play?"

"Well, none, right now. I don't have one. But, I do listen to the Royal Musicians whenever I can."

"Do you think you could play an instrument if you had one?"

"Of course, if I had one."

At his answer, Neppam turned his attention to the gurgling stream splashing around the rocks. The water caught a clump of dried grass and pulled it into its bubbling flow. Neppam rose swiftly and moved into the gold light of the morning sun spreading its fullness across the landscape. The morning breeze rustled the soft fabric of his robe as he parted the grass with his confident stride.

James ran in the opposite direction toward Poule. He stopped once to look back at him. Neppam's strong physique cut the light of the rising sun. He raised his staff to wave.

After returning from the Ansling Hills, Neppam directed his servant, Kalem, to look for an instrument for James. It proved a difficult task. The few who owned instruments in the surrounding villages refused to part with them. Kalem returned empty handed. Undaunted, Neppam sent him north to the Castle Yves.

The Castle Yves was a unique conglomerate of buildings and courtyards designed to house the queen and her royal court. The inner courtyards were meticulously connected by finely sculpted lawns and gardens. The median housed businesses that supported the missions of the noblemen who ruled Fiara. The outer yard was lined with workshops where instruments and tools for the Royal Order of Artists were made.

Kalem bought his way into the outer courtyard. The coin from Neppam's pouch jangled along his waist as he walked along the line of guitars displayed in one of the workshops. The craftsmen at Yves were shrewd, but Kalem had experience in dealing with them. When he left the Castle Yves, it was with a refurbished guitar of exquisite tone and quality; and he still had a few coins left jangling in his pouch.

Neppam gave the guitar as a gift to James. The boy cherished it, carrying it wherever he went. James tried to imitate the Royal Musicians who played in Poule. He sat for hours by himself playing and practicing, until he finally created his own music. One day, he found the courage to visit Neppam and play his songs for him.

Neppam absently sucked in his cheeks attempting to rekindle the dead ashes of his pipe. The waning warmth from the morning fire mingled with the approaching heat of noonday. It created a heavy, thick atmosphere in the room. His breathing came slowly. He closed his eyes, listening to the music filling the room, and smiled when the sound broke in the middle of a phrase.

"I'm still listening, James."

"I thought you were asleep."

"No, I hear the notes better with my eyes closed."

Neppam shifted in his chair while the boy engaged in another piece of music. It was an original love song. Simple and innocent, it captured Neppam's heart.

"He is more than talented. He is gifted," Neppam thought. "He is ready to enter the Royal Order of Musicians."

Neppam shuddered. James was young. He could lose himself in the regimen of the royal court. Neppam hoped his gift could grow unspoiled. He leaned forward.

"You play well, James. I like your music. You know how to play guitar. It's amazing that you taught yourself." He let the words sink into the boy. "How would you like to learn piano?"

"I don't have a piano."

"I know someone who does."

"Who?"

"Mrs. Winthrop."

"Mrs. Winthrop? She's strange."

"I'm surprised at you, James."

"That's what everyone says."

Neppam tapped the bowl of his pipe into the palm of his hand and blew the ashes into the air. He laid the pipe on a nearby table. "You're afraid of her."

"No."

"Good. I want you to talk with her today."

Mrs. Winthrop stood on the tips of her toes, stirring the large kettle of soup. She sputtered and stewed as she pulled a stool into place and climbed to reach a bottle of seasoning. She sprinkled a pinch of seasoning into the broth and dipped a spoon, twirling the contents thoroughly. As she lifted a taste into her mouth, she cocked her ear to a soft rapping sound. Dropping the spoon in haste, she ran to answer the door. She stopped for a moment, smoothed her apron and brushed back the wisps of her hair, then opened the door to James timidly waiting on the threshold.

Mrs. Winthrop looked up and down the street and in a troubled voice said, "I'm sorry, but there is no one at home."

"What about you?"

"Me?" Her eyes moistened. "Well, you may come in if you like."

She led him into the sitting room and offered him a seat on the sofa. An upright piano hugged the wood of a wall in the room. Mrs. Winthrop went to the piano, dusting the keys with the palm of her hand.

"This was Mr. Jacob's," she warmly cooed. "He loved to play." Her expression suddenly turned cold. "I'll make tea," she excused herself and disappeared into the kitchen.

Mrs. Winthrop was leery of youngsters. It was a trait born from harassment and ridicule. To avoid confrontation and pain, she confined herself to the home Mr. Jacob had bequeathed her. She often dreamed that he still moved about in the study or walked quietly in the fresh dew of the garden. If she closed her eyes, she sometimes could hear his footsteps in the next room. She could feel him swoop past her and seat himself at the piano bench.

She lightly closed her eyes as the tea seeped and she started to hum. She gingerly picked up the tray and carried it into the living room to serve James. They quietly sipped tea for a few moments.

"Tell me. What is your name?"

"My name is James McCautry. I live at the edge of the village with my family."

She nodded her head, recognizing the name. "And what can I do for you, James?"

"I want you to teach me piano."

"You have a piano?"

"Oh, no, I want to use your piano."

"No. I don't let anyone play it."

"But I need to learn how to play piano. It's the only one in Poule."

"I said no. I don't let anyone play it." Her heart softened only a little when his eyes glazed with disappointment. "Please, understand. Anything that was Mr. Jacob's is very precious to me. It's all I have left of him, and it won't last forever. You understand?"

"I'm sorry I bothered you," James tried to hide his hurt feelings as he got up and left.

Mrs. Winthrop heard the door click. She rose and went to the window. Clouds gathered in the wind, swirling in angry clusters across the afternoon sky. She remembered James as she greeted him for the first time at the door, his excited look when she showed him the piano and his glazed, hurt eyes when she refused to help him. A shudder passed through her. She felt lonely and wondered why her life had grown so empty.

Tears welled in her eyes and her heart ached.

As the clouds overcame the last corner of blue sky, she gathered her wrap and went out the front door looking for the young boy, James.

Neppam paced back and forth within the sitting room. The wood in the fireplace crackled and popped with the heat of the fire.

"What's keeping him?"

"I don't know. Perhaps it's a good sign," Mrs. Winthrop adjusted herself, heaving a sigh. "Maybe he went home."

Neppam scowled. "He said he would come here first."

"Then, he'll come." Mrs. Winthrop brushed her lap. "I don't see why you're so upset. You've been scowling since he first mentioned auditioning for the royal court. He's worked hard for this opportunity. It's a chance for a better life for him and a chance to fulfill his dreams."

"Yes, I suppose so, but there isn't anything wrong with village life. Everyone makes a fuss over the royal court, but for some, it's only a glittering trap that squeezes the life from their souls." Neppam stopped pacing, interrupted by the subtle creaking of the front door.

James slipped into the room. He set his guitar down and scuffed a foot. "I thought it went well. I think they liked me."

"Of course, they liked you. They have ears." Mrs. Winthrop nodded her head in assurance.

"They didn't like me enough. They said to try again next year."

"Next year? That's what they said?" Neppam frowned in disbelief.

"That's what they said." James lowered his eyes watching his feet closely. The silence stunned him. He lifted his toe, rocking the guitar case ever so slightly. He reached for the handle and lifted his instrument as he turned toward the door. "Don't worry. I won't give up." He left before they could say a word.

Throughout the night, he wandered through the fields that surrounded his village. Numb and disenchanted, his dwindling hope stung him repeatedly like a heated prong. By morning, he returned home, packed his knapsack and headed across the grassy plains, leaving Poule far behind in the gathering dawn.

3

The city streets of Sumatra pulsated with activity on the second evening of the Festival of Reanoke. People, from as far away as Ishna, Murlock and Hamerton, roamed the streets in search of entertainment. The displays and booths lining the main thoroughfare bustled with noise. Merchants and vendors and men of the games called to the crowd in excited anticipation as it ebbed and swirled past them. Amid the din and confusion, members of theatrical companies worked feverishly to complete preparations for the next day's performance. The sound of their hammers punctuated the night air, rhythmically accenting the flow of people along the city streets. The presence of these visitors nearly doubled the city's population.

James felt the gnawing impetus as he pulled the travois with the old man, Tabum, through the boisterous crowd. The handles of the travois bit into his blistered hands. John maneuvered ahead of him, pushing and shoving, clearing a path for the old man. His raw language drifted in sharp, broken phrases that grated against the evening sky.

When they reached the main square of the city, they went to the Belshire Tavern where they were scheduled to play for the festival. The owner of the tavern turned them away. They were late. He was too busy to argue the point with them. They let the stream of people swallow them and pushed against the flow of the current, until they reached the edge of the square. There, they were propelled several streets beyond to where the crowd thinned.

James eased the travois to the ground. As they looked around the area, John spotted an outdoor café. "I could stand a drink or two," he said.

"Not until we find a room," James spit the words out in a terse growl. His body ached and his hands were torn from carrying the heavy load.

"Don't worry. I have friends here. We'll find a place to stay." John helped him pull the old man through the crowded streets towards the lake shore.

The shore that trimmed the city of Sumatra was decorated with the remains of grand homes that once had served as summer retreats for the wealthy families of Fiara. Worn and tattered, like old garments discarded at the end of a fruitful season of pleasure, they hugged the land with nostalgic whimsy. The familiar elegance of their rich design now was converted to house the weary travelers and rousing drunks who moved through the city on their way to impressive destinations.

The Ishtosh house overlooked the fishing docks of Sumatra. It was a dilapidated old home with ample rooms. A necessary neglect was reflected in its weather-beaten exterior and shadowed character. Its heritage was etched in every worn shingle and sagging abutment. Ena Ishtosh was a part of its unusual appeal. She was a daughter of a fisherman who had abandoned his meager fortune for the rugged charm of the distinctive home. Ena was known by those who scavenged the waterfront for food or a dry place to spend a cold and damp night. Her sharp wit eased the trouble of the day and her generosity warmed their hearts, lighting the dark corners in their souls, a darkness caused by deprivation.

Ena was bathing when a relentless pounding summoned her. She cussed as she scrambled to cover her round figure with a robe, flooding the room with her hasty departure. Lumbering through the hall, her annoyance kindled with every step. The cool night air, whisking along her damp body, fanned her irritation. When she reached the front entrance, she defiantly opened the door only a crack.

"We're full up, so be on your way."

"Hold on now, Madame." John swiftly struggled to keep the door ajar. "Don't turn me away."

"Oh, you think I won't." Ena scowled as John forced his way into the foyer. "I see you still have quite the nerve."

"I have." John lightheartedly clasped his arms around her in a warm hug and swung her around the entranceway.

"I want to finish my bath, John. I haven't time to listen to you. You have your own motives for knocking on my door.

This time, I haven't any room for you. It's the festival. The rooms are filled."

"Oh, Ena, we've nowhere else to go. You've got to have something for us."

"I do? I'm supposed to have a room saved for you? John will be in town for the festival. I better save him some space. This time you're asking for more than even your fine tongue can conjure. No room. I'm sorry."

"Ena, we've a poor, dying man out there. He's got to have some rest. I'm not lying this time. I've someone who really needs your help."

Ena eyed John in suspicion. Wrapping herself tighter in her robe, she went to a window and lifted a corner of the curtain. Through the evening shadows she saw James stooping next to a handmade carrier. In the dark, she could barely make out the figure of a man lying in the travois. She watched as James lifted a canteen trying to help him drink.

"Oh, all right," Ena softened, warmth invading her stern face. She let the curtain drop. "Let them in. I've one room left. It's small, mind you. It's nothing even a beggar would want."

John flourished a bow to her in respect, and then he left to help James pull the carrier into the house.

When Ena opened the door to their room, John groaned at the small quarters. Ignoring him, Ena entered the cramped room and lit a lamp. The light brought little warmth to the sparse furnishings of the room. Ena stepped aside as they eased the old man onto the bed. While they covered him with the thin bedcover, Ena left the room. She returned with a soft, thick blanket in her hands.

"This will keep the chill from him," she said placing it at the end of the bed.

As she made her way back down the hall, John grumbled loudly at her back, "It's hardly big enough for one person, let alone all of us."

"I keep it only for emergencies," Ena retorted over her shoulder.

"For punishment," John spit out the words in a yell. He watched her disappear around a corner in the hallway. "Well, it'll have to do for now. I'll fix it up with the Belshire owner and then we'll be out of here."

"The festival will be through in a few days," James reminded him. He dropped to the floor at the edge of the bed.

"So, we play for a few days. That's all we need for the Queen's producers to hear us."

James tugged at the bedcovers, his eyes filling with doubt. "You heard him, John. He said we were too late. He's replaced us."

"Come on, James. So, we're a little late. You don't think he really found anyone to replace us? He's just mad at us. I've talked us out of worse trouble than this. Tonight, I'll talk us right back into a job. You'll see. You stay with the old fellow."

Before James could protest, John slipped out the door and made his way out of the house. James stared at the closed door. His stomach rolled. His muscles tensed.

"He's confident." The whispery voice distanced James from his gnawing feelings of frustration.

"Yes," James turned to the old man. "He's confident."

Tabum closed his eyes. His chin dropped in exhaustion. James cradled his own head in the crook of his arms, resting them against his knees. He felt relieved as his mind relaxed in the darkness of his lids. The damp air from Lake Tazia tickled his nostrils as he drew in deep, rhythmic breaths that gently lulled him toward a quiet sleep.

"I haven't much time."

The earnest tone wretched James from his rest. He brought his head upright, "You'll be all right. Can I get you something, some food or something to drink?"

"No." Tabum drew his lips together, squinting with distaste.

James studied him. He looked pale and sallow, his brow furrowed with discomfort. He smoothed the bedcovers, pulling them under Tabum's chin. As he did, a tear escaped Tabum. It slithered along the depression under his eye, fanning into a glistening sheet that wet his cheek. James released the bedcover feeling accused.

"We haven't much money left. We need to work the festival. After the festival is over, I'll take you anywhere you want to go."

Tabum's eyes remained closed. His brow crinkled again. When the old man finally fell asleep, James found a spot on the floor and, using his knapsack as a pillow, he settled in for the night. For a long while, he lay awake, listening for Tabum's breath against the night air.

Sometime during the night, James awakened. John still had not returned. Uneasily, James rose and went to Tabum's bedside, reaching to extinguish the lamp. As he did, he noticed that Tabum gripped the end of a necklace hanging around his neck. In his sleep, Tabum's hand relaxed gently releasing the necklace. James saw a crystal in the shape of a wing hanging from a gold chain. The crystal wing was jagged along one side, as if a piece had been torn from it. The light from the lamp refracted in the crystal creating a rainbow of colors. Its eerie glow captured James. He stared at it, finding it difficult to break away from its beauty.

Tabum gripped the wing again in his sleep. James stepped back alarmed, expecting him to awaken. The old man lay quiet, holding the crystal wing tightly in his fist.

James returned to the cold floor. He tossed and turned, trying to sleep. His mind raced with questions about the crystal wing. As James lingered in the twilight between consciousness and sleep, he thought he heard a rustle coming from the bed—a rapid stirring in the room, like the sound of a great bird beating its wings against the night air. He called out in fear to Tabum.

The sound of his voice was met by a deep silence.

4

John tugged across the hollow of his cheekbone in frustration. Ben Dang was stubborn. The Belshire Tavern owner had too much money invested in the festival to let John convince him to change his venue again to accommodate him. They had been replaced. He refused to reconsider. Ben brought ale to the table and placed it casually in front of John as appeasement. John ordered a whiskey to chase it. He glared at the ale and whiskey as if seeking vengeance in its amber color and harsh taste. His face burned with anger. When he thought of returning to the boarding house with his news, a knot welled, twisting and swelling in his chest. No, he would not tell James now. He ordered another drink.

The noise from a nearby table disrupted his sullen thoughts. "Pipe down," he exploded in irritation.

"Oh, excuse us," a snotty voice confronted him. A young man bolted from his chair and gave an exaggerated, unbalanced bow. He pulled himself upright and assumed a victorious stance, looking down his nose arrogantly at John. His companions burst into laughter.

With a swift assault, John forced the youth back into his seat. His companions rose quickly to assist him. As they got up, John struck the table with his fists, vibrating wood and glass. "I wouldn't do that if I were you."

The men backed into their seats, wary of his rugged body and imposing, dark sneer. One cautioned John. "Hold on now. There's no need for violence. We're here for a good time, that's all."

"At my expense," John targeted the man, barely controlling his rage.

"Of course not," the man spoke calmly. "The lad didn't mean any harm. He's had a little too much to drink. If it troubles you, we better settle it quietly." He gently paused and added, "For our sake."

John turned an empty chair around and straddled it. "You're a smart man," he laughed.

"My name is Boyden." The man offered a hand in friendship to John.

"Mine is John. You're all right, Boyden, but that one needs a swift kick."

"Tom? I apologize for him. He's drunk. I hope you won't hold it against us," Boyden nudged the fellow sitting next to him. "This is Eric. A group of us are visiting for the festival.

We're all musicians, but we're not playing this time around. We're here to listen."

"I'm a musician, too. My partner and I were scheduled to play here, until Ben Dang got too gnarly for our taste. We were a little late, you see, with a good excuse. The man has no compassion."

"I know the man," Boyden nodded. "He doesn't take kindly to the tardy. If you don't show on time, he replaces you. No excuses accepted."

"I was depending on this engagement to get us an audition with the Queen's producers. I heard there would be quite a few producers scouting for talent at the festival. It doesn't happen too often anymore."

Boyden uneasily glanced at John. "You've a mind to enter the Royal Order of Musicians?"

"I can taste it."

"It might be tough. I understand they look down on troubadours."

"It doesn't matter. We're good enough to change their minds," John leaned forward onto his forearms.

"I don't know, John. You may be good enough to change their minds, but I don't think producers are looking for talent when they come here. They are looking for drink." Boyden toyed with his glass. "Why don't you forget about it for now and enjoy yourself. Maybe, we'll come up with something better than playing in this tavern."

"Like what?" John sarcastically glinted.

"I don't know," Boyden dodged his question. He studied John in an irksome silence. "I'm bored with this place. Come back to our rooms with us and play a few songs. I want to see how good you really are."

John's lips tightened into a sardonic tilt with the challenge. He reached for his glass without removing his eyes from Boyden and finished the drink in one gulp. "Let's go."

John and the men left the tavern and hurried through the dark streets to a hotel in the central plaza of Sumatra. Sculptured gardens decorated the reflective pools garnishing the entrance to the hotel where the men were staying. As they passed the sentry on duty, John let out an uneasy whistle. "You must have a patron to stay here."

"Yes, we do. We've had good luck," Boyden said nonchalantly. He led them through the lobby and up the broad, elegant staircase to the second floor. While inserting a key into the lock of his suite door, he turned from John to the other men. "I'd like this to be a duo."

With a question highlighting his face, Eric guided Tom away from the door and down the hall. John walked into the suite and briskly took a turn around the sitting room, admiring the lavish furnishings. "Impressive."

Boyden pointed to several guitars resting in a corner of the room. "You choose first."

John examined each guitar by touching, holding and moving the inside of his palms over the instrument. When he finally selected one, Boyden went to his bedroom emerging with his own instrument. As they warmed up, John watched as Boyden's fingers flew swiftly along the guitar neck, eventually molding the exercises into a complicated musical arrangement. John dove in accompanying him with ease. In the heat of playing, Boyden asked, "Do you write your own?" John nodded and improvised a musical transition into one of his own songs.

"You wrote that?" Boyden mused, "It's good." He let his guitar rest on the floor in front of him as John began to sing. "You've got a good voice. It's easy to listen to."

A knock on the door interrupted them. Tom stuck his head into the room. "Boyd, it's been a long while. We'd like to join you."

"You can come in now, Tom." Boyden waved his hand beckoning him into the room and then turned to John. "I promised them a party. You won't mind if we stop now. I've heard enough, anyways."

John put the guitar down, suppressing his irritation. He watched as the room swarmed with people and chatter overtook the air in the suite. While someone tapped a cask of ale, Tom brought out glasses from a cupboard. John watched the scene unfolding before him in silent consternation.

Eric kept John and Boyden in his view, making his way across the room to smilingly confront them, "You were in here too long." He nodded to Boyden as he spoke. "He must be good."

"He's good." Boyden motioned toward Tom. "Tell Tom to get the brew."

Eric raised his eyes in disbelief, but approached Tom and whispered in his ear. "The brew," Tom chirped in agitated surprise.

"Yes. That's what I said."

Tom left the room. When he returned, he carried a large silver decanter with decorative gold overlays. He circled the room, diligently serving a select portion of the guests. When he finished filling the glasses, Boyden lifted his glass in a toast to John. "I welcome you to our group."

As John lifted his glass to his lips to drink, he heard a snide voice jeer, "He's a troubadour." The degrading tone sparked his temper. He placed his glass on a table without tasting the drink and turned to leave the party. "Nice party, Boyd."

"Wait." Eric grabbed his arm as he tried to leave. "Overlook what was said. Not everyone approves of you here."

"I'm heartbroken," John mocked Eric's appeal. "I don't need approval from any of you."

"You do if you are going to play with us."

"Why would I want to play with you? My partner and I do fine alone."

A hush fell over the group. Eric turned to Boyden in confusion. "You didn't tell him."

"I didn't tell him. You didn't give me time."

"Tell me what?"

Boyden laughed. "I'm afraid I owe you an apology, John. I never intended to help you. I thought you were boasting about your musical expertise. I brought you here intending to embarrass you. You know. Show you up. You surprised me. You are excellent. I really enjoy your music and appreciate your ability."

Eric struck a note of confidence, "Boyden is a producer, John. Our patron is the Queen."

Boyden handed John his glass. "It's called Grogg. Only members of the court are allowed to drink it. Go ahead. Drink it."

"You are saying that I am a member of the court? I'm in? I am a Royal Musician?"

"Yes, that is what I am saying. Go on and drink it."

John smelled the delicate aroma of the brew wafting into each breath he took and asked, "And my partner?"

"We'll consider him if he's as good as you."

"I wouldn't work with him if he wasn't as good as me."

Boyden chuckled, "Then he doesn't have anything to worry about. I'll listen to him tomorrow."

John slowly looked around the group with a discerning eye, and then swallowed every drop of the Royal Brew.

Under the influence of the Grogg, the distance from the hotel to the Ishtosh house seemed to take an eternity. John didn't mind the delay. The effervescent glow of the rising sun cast bright colored hues against the sides of the buildings and jogged his creative soul. John noticed every detail of the surfaces it touched. Every one of his senses seemed heightened, sharpened to the greatest clarity. He wandered the quiet streets of Sumatra humming snatches of melodies he loved. When he reached the Ishtosh house, the silence from the very spaces between the houses nearby seemed to rush him. He entered the house and groped his way down the hall to his room. With each step he took, his excitement mounted. He could not wait any longer to tell James the good news. Their long sought journey to enter the court was culminating into success. By evening, they both would be members of the Royal Order of Musicians. John steadied himself before turning the knob of the door to their room. When he turned it fully, the door opened into the hollowness of an empty room.

5

Fate has a way of ensuring success, Tabum thought. Strength of conviction blossomed from the deep well of his soul. He moved his hand resting it over his breast pocket. Underneath the cloth, his finger felt the shape of the crystal wing. He had waited a long time. He had looked even longer. A smile lit his weary face. There was no need to dispose of the wing now. He had found James. James was the one for whom he had searched.

Tabum turned on his side, grimacing. His pain reminded him of his difficult life and his struggle to keep the crystal wing a secret. It had belonged to his mother. All her life, she guarded it as if it were a forbidden treasure. She told Tabum the wing helped her find fortune and warned him that no one must ever know. He never saw the wing. To him, it was only a fanciful tale woven by a gentle and creative woman, who somehow managed to support him in quiet splendor in a world darkened by greed and strife.

She waited until he reached maturity before she took him into the dense woods next to their home and showed him the crystal wing. Hidden within the deep forest, she let him use it for the first time. With authority and patience, she guided him, telling him all she had learned about its use, warning him of the grave responsibility of owning it.

"The wing touches in here," she said pointing to her heart. "But it also touches out here," she opened her hands to the air. "Within and without—it's all connected. You must always use it for good. The wing has been taken away from its source. Away from its source, it is in danger. So let the wing take you. It knows where it must go."

Tabum heeded her words. For many years, his life was peaceful, filled with the delight of discovery and the comfort of wealth. One day, the wing gave him warning. A man was looking for it. How he had learned of it, Tabum did not know. He only knew what his heart told him. The man was a danger to him and the crystal wing. Without question, Tabum abandoned his estate, taking only a few coins and the crystal wing. Within the despair of the lonely streets of the cities and the humble poverty of the rural folks, Tabum hid his treasure from the man of darkness who haunted his dreams.

Tabum lived the rest of his long adult life wandering the countryside from the Arca V'ing Enta to the Sea of Abyss. He lived as a pauper, circulating among the lost and deprived in Fiara. Whenever the wing prompted him, he journeyed to the Arca V'ing Enta; and when the wing prompted him again, he moved inland away from its force. He always searched for someone he could entrust with the crystal wing. As he advanced further with age, his strength waned; and he began his final walk to the Sea of Abyss, where he planned to give the crystal wing a safe and final resting place.

Tabum cringed as he felt warm water dribble along his groin and spread across the backside of his legs. He closed his eyes as he felt the burning chafe of the moisture against his skin. When he opened his eyes again, James sat next to the campfire, sniffing the night air, his trance broken by the acrid smell of urine.

James removed the urine soaked pants. He pulled a fresh cloth from his knapsack, swabbed Tabum's skin and tucked a dry blanket around him. James lay back against his knapsack, the strain of his concern lining the corners of his eyes. He heaved a sigh filled with sorrow and regret. Tabum's heart reached out in sympathy for him.

His sight blurred as he absorbed the emotional pain he sensed from James. He reached into his pocket removing the crystal wing. "One more time," he thought, slipping the chain over his head.

A glimmer of light reflecting off the wing attracted James to Tabum's side. He reached out to touch it. "What is it?" he whispered. The old man intercepted his hand. Tabum did not answer. His lids drooped. James stayed close to the old man. The light from the wing mesmerized him.

"You like it, don't you?" Tabum said without opening his eyes.

"Uh, why yes. I've never seen anything like it."

"There is not another like it in Fiara. It's been handed down in my family for generations. Go ahead. Take it," Tabum slipped his fingers under the chain and gave the wing to James.

Cupping the wing in his hand, James ran his fingers over its shape. "It looks damaged."

"Yes. It happened a long time ago. It's still a beautiful piece. It's a crystal wing."

"It's beautiful," James held the wing out to Tabum.

"No. I'd like you to keep it."

"I couldn't. You said it's been handed down..."

"I'm the last in my line, James. No one will miss it." Tabum closed James's hand around the wing. "Go on. Keep it in a safe place. Tell no one about it. When we reach the sea, I'll tell you more about it." Tabum closed his eyes, succumbing to his fatigue.

James framed the wing with the flesh of his palm and placed it inside his knapsack. After securing the pack, he laid out his bedroll and tried to fall asleep.

In the morning, he burned the urine soaked cloths in the fire and refilled their canteens from a nearby stream. Throughout the day, he pulled the travois across Fiara's landscape until they reached the lush fields of Eastham. There, they headed east for several days, until the pungent, saline aroma of the warm breeze teased him. He accelerated his pace. When he reached the top of a grassy crest in the land, he came to an abrupt halt.

The sun pushed velvet shades of red and gold along the edges of the horizon. It tinted the landscape with its soothing aura, brushing against the sky. Before him, the Sea of Abyss lay dormant, mirroring the fiery colors of the setting sun. A smooth, wet tidal surface lined its shore. Its calm bulk seemed endless, expansive, as if invisible barriers held it from spilling over to cover the world.

"We made it," James said overcome by the breathtaking vista of the sea. He laid the carrier on the ground. As he did, his sight moved along the body of the old man. A hollow ache gathered in his chest and spread into his throat as he wondered how long it had been since the old man had released his final breath. He trembled as he kneeled beside the lifeless body, touching the old man's hands with compassion. The hands were cold. James moved his hand over the old man's chest, smoothed the clothing, and pulled the blanket over the body. He thought how peaceful and natural death looked. He began to shiver, and in the eerie stillness of approaching evening, he quietly wept.

James had never seen death. He didn't know what to do with the body, and didn't have tools to dig a grave, so he built a fire on the crest of the hill overlooking the sea waiting for morning to break. As dusk gave way to darkness, he huddled close to the fire. The sight of the body disturbed him. Memories of his early days in Poule haunted his mind. He fought a building sense of hopelessness. Before morning, he went to the old man's body and strapped it to the travois. Guiding the travois down the damp slope, he placed it into the muddy shore.

When the first hint of day lit the horizon, Abyss stirred. Its smooth surface exploded into seething waves. The waves rushed in torrents filling the jagged bowl of the shoreline. James climbed the bank, fighting the violent assault of the sea. It hurled him against the embankment until his skin bruised and ripped. As he struggled to safety, James looked back. He saw the old man spewed into the air and devoured by the jowls of the sea.

Drenched and frightened, James fell exhausted onto the bank along the edge of the sea. He lay prostrate for hours in the coarse grass. The image of the old man tossing within the waves filled his mind, while the mournful howl of the wind carried him into sleep. When he awoke, his mind felt clouded and tight. The sun hung low in the sky. He stared across the face of the sea for a long while. Stormy winds lashed his body. The grass whipped his face. When the sun disappeared behind the vast swell of water, James gathered his knapsack and began the long journey back to Sumatra.

6

"Well, one of you finally decided to show your face around here again. By rights, I should call in the law; but I'll settle for money instead. Come on, young man. Cough it up." Ena twitched the palm of her outstretched hand in annoyance.

"Didn't John settle with you?"

"John? You're joking, of course; and I'm not in a mind to laugh. Just hand it over."

"All right, all right." James searched his knapsack, depositing the money he found into Ena's hand.

"Is that all you've got! This won't even cover half the use of the room."

"I swear. John handled all our finances."

"Your finances, indeed. Check your pockets. Go on. There might be more in there." Ena poked James and helped him turn out his pockets.

"Are you satisfied? I haven't any more."

"It figures," Ena scowled as she slipped the coins into her pocket. "Well, until you come by the rest, you'll have to work for a living. You can have the front room upstairs. And this," she jingled the coins in her pocket. "This will be the deposit on the room. The rest, you still owe me."

"I didn't plan on staying in Sumatra, Ena."

"And I didn't plan on losing money. I lost plenty this festival with clients suddenly developing a case of the poor or conveniently disappearing when it come time to pay. No, you'll stay in Sumatra and pay this one off. It won't take long for you to earn the balance."

"But, Ena, I need to look for John. He probably thinks I skipped out on him."

"Well, I know you both did on me. So, I should get first consideration."

James studied her set jaw line. She faltered only slightly in her adamant stare. He shrugged, smirking in agreement. "I suppose, I could spend some time here, if I can find work."

Ena made her way to the reception desk crowded in a corner of the foyer. "You'll find work. If not, I've plenty to do around here." She tossed James a set of keys and, with pleasure, watched him reluctantly ascend the front stairway.

When James arrived at his room, he threw his knapsack into a corner and looked around the room. It was so different from the one they had occupied during the festival. The bed was covered with a comforter. Its patches were filled with yellows, gold, and wheat, and trimmed with fine lines in black. Several white linen pillows lay over the colors at the head of the bed. On the left side of the room, a dark wood bureau stood against the wall. Its carved polished trim contrasted the smooth white surface. Soft, blue tapestry hung along the sides of glass doors leading to a balcony running the length of the room. To the right of the doors, a wood table supported a glass lantern. The lantern was large enough to provide ample light for the room.

James bounced on the double bed, testing it before settling into its inviting comfort. The numbing fingers of exhaustion ran across the edges of his muscles and tickled his tongue to its root. He drew in a heavy breath. Feelings of loneliness overcame him. John's disappearance intensified the growing vacancy eating at his heart. He wondered what his journey to the sea had accomplished. The old man had died. John was gone. His tongue thickened and his throat tightened as he fought to quell his rising despair.

The sun reflecting from Lake Tazia's water glinted off the glass surface of the balcony doors. The warm hues cast into the room from the setting sun calmed the ravaging ache within him. James watched the light flicker. It reminded him of the light from the crystal wing. With a feeling of restlessness, he went to his pack, searching it for the wing. When he found it, he lay on the bed, holding it high, swinging it back and forth. He turned it to various angles. There wasn't a sign of light. The wing remained clear. Disappointment pushed its way into his thoughts. In spite of its alluring beauty, it was only a damaged crystal—a broken wing.

James placed the wing around his neck. As he listened to the distant sound of waves licking the wharf beneath his balcony doors, he drifted into an unsettled rest. As James rested, his ears caught snatches of voices from fishermen guiding their boats into dock. Their rustic bantering billowed and swirled in his mind, propelling him into a magnetic darkness. From within the darkness, a bright light shone. It blinded him.

As his eyes adjusted to the intense light, James saw an outline of natural rock. Within the sculpted arms of the rock was a jewel, too large for a man to carry. James was unable to approach the jewel. He moved away from it, trying to avert its pervasive light, and descended into a grassy clearing. From the clearing, James could see the slope of the meadow. The edge of the meadow met a silhouette of a forbidding, massive stone wall. From the height of the mountain, he glimpsed the sparkling lights of a distant city, twinkling across the water of a lake far below him. He watched the city lights, until he was compelled to return to the jewel.

The jewel drew him closer. When its light completely encompassed him, it diffused. James was able to finally see the setting holding the jewel. At the base of the jewel lay a crystal wing. Emblazoned into the stone next to the wing was an imprint of another wing. James reached out, trying to touch the stone. A force pulled him away. His heart rapidly beat against his chest. He labored to catch his breath.

"This is the last time I call you, James. You can go hungry for all I care after this," Ena pounded on the door once, giving her words emphasis.

James's tongue dragged against the inside of his dry mouth as he tried to part his lips to answer her. He was unable to funnel his breath into sound. His body felt weighted. It threatened to suffocate him. In weakness, he lifted a hand, trying to call for help. Her footsteps stomped away from his door. His heart fluttered. He stymied his fear.

As James lay in the dusk, the evening breeze moved forcefully across the balcony doors, rattling the glass panes. When the wind gusted, he experienced a refreshing surge of energy that broke his suffering. As strength spread through him, he pulled himself onto his side and sat up, dangling his legs over the edge of the bed until his head cleared.

James removed the crystal wing from his neck. The warm touch of the crystal on his cool hand brought him to the brink of edginess. Closing his fist around the wing, he pressed it into his thigh in frustration. He felt confused. The mountain with its jewel seemed so real. Resisting an impulse to throw the wing over the balcony into the water of Lake Tazia, James deposited the wing into the pocket of his knapsack and went downstairs. He found Ena in a back pantry.

"I saved you a plate." Ena pointed to a dish on the sideboard.

"Thanks, but I don't feel hungry."

"Eat anyways." Ena handed the plate to him. "Don't worry. I won't charge you for it."

James took the plate. He nibbled at the food as he talked. "I thought I'd look around this evening and see if anyone could use a musician. Have you any idea of a good place to start?"

"There are several places that might be looking for someone, but you'd make more money, faster, if you'd hire on at the docks."

"No, I couldn't do that. I'm not a fisherman."

Ena laughed, "But you've a good strong back and your muscles are young. They'd make use of you."

"No, I better not," he drawled, unsure.

"You can plan on staying for some time, then. The pay for musicians after the festival is pitiful."

"No worse than I've made before, I'm sure. Besides, I haven't anywhere to go, and no one to go with."

"What happened to the old man you left with?"

"He's dead," James's voice grew husky. He stopped eating.

"I'm so sorry. I should have guessed as much." Ena reached out to pet his hand.

"It's all right. I didn't know him very well. I did grow attached to him, though, traveling like that."

"And you haven't any idea where John could have gone to?" Ena busied her hands by stacking dishes into a cupboard.

"No. We hadn't made plans for after the festival. I thought he'd wait for me."

"You'll run into him. John always turns up in Sumatra, eventually." Ena lowered her head, hiding the sympathy she felt for James. "There's a tavern three doors down from here. I know the owner. He sometimes uses musicians after the festival is over. You can tell him I sent you."

James set his unfinished plate onto the sideboard. "Thanks, Ena. My first pay will go to you."

"It most certainly will. And several after that, I'll remind you."

After leaving Ena, James gathered his instrument from his room and made his way along the dimly lit waterfront to the Mogire Tavern. The Mogire sat nestled in thick shrubs between several rooming houses. Its simple design defied the elaborate architecture of the other houses along the shore of Sumatra and its well-kept exterior testified to its popularity with the citizens of Sumatra.

James carried his instrument up the front stairs leading to the verandah of the house. At the top of the steps, he was intercepted by a burly young man who directed him to a door at the back of the house. At the back door, James was greeted by a young woman dressed for kitchen work. She showed him to a stool at the corner of the hearth and asked him to wait.

Longley Mogire huffed into the kitchen tearing a linen napkin from underneath his chin. He screwed his face into a scowl when he saw James. "I guessed it was another musician. I understand Ena Ishtosh sent you. It's the only reason I'll bother with you. You want a job, I suppose." He noticed his instrument. "I can't use a guitarist. I need someone who plays piano."

"I play piano," James assured him.

"You are a troubadour who plays piano? That's interesting. I'll try you tonight, then. I said try. You'll have to be good for me to consider hiring you." Mogire ran his sight across his clothing. "You're dressed a little ragged for our establishment. I'll overlook it tonight. Wait back here until I send for you. And don't bother anyone. I pay them to work, not chatter."

James waited for several hours in the kitchen before Mogire sent an associate to get him. The tavern room was filled to capacity with affluent citizens from the area. A grand piano graced a corner of the elegant room. James's eyes lit at the sight of it.

Mogire joined James at the piano. "Be good to it," he warned. "They're hard to come by. I had to use influence to get this one." Mogire rubbed the polished wood with his fingers as James began to play. At the expressive, passionate sound of the keyboard, Mogire looked up in delight. "Excellent," he thumped his hand on the piano case. "Where did you learn to play? Never mind. Keep playing." Mogire returned to his table. When the last customer straggled from the tavern, he arranged the conditions for James's employment.

Over the next few weeks, the days fell into a comfortable routine. James rose late in the morning. After having lunch with Ena, he wandered the shoreline of Lake Tazia finding a secluded spot to practice his guitar. In late afternoon, James went back to the Ishtosh house where he waited for the fishing boats to dock from their daily excursion upon the lake. He spent the last hour before going to work with the men who sailed the lake each day.

Once in a while, in the twilight hours after he returned from work, he removed the crystal wing from its hiding place and lay in the soft comfort of his bedroom with the wing around his neck. Each time he did, he soared to the mountain with its jewel of light, awakening always in physical discomfort, but always with the feeling something had been given to him.

Using the wing in the peaceful lakeside community, James rejuvenated his creativity. He composed new songs and reorganized the priorities in his life. Over time, his ambitions cooled. As if by instinct, he kept the crystal wing a secret, rebelling against the practical sense that told him the wing was an ordinary necklace and the jewel an imaginative dream.

7

Kate grew impatient as the workmen fixed her coach. The sun burned the dusty road underneath her feet. Its blistering rays toasted the delicate threads of her dress. She fanned the warm air around her face with her hand, leaning against the coach and ignoring the disapproving glances of her companions. As the hour wore on, she grew restless and irritable. Perspiration trickled down her back, altering the softness of her fine garb into a wet bulk. The material clung to her skin, abrading her. With caustic vehemence, she commented on the slow progress of the workers, until she moved to the refuge of the cool forest in exasperation. Several members of her group tried to follow her.

"No, I'm going alone," she dismissed them. She walked through the dense flora and took a seat on the surface of a large rock protruding from the ground. She stretched enjoying the cool sensation along her buttocks, listening to the rustle of leaves as her travel companions wandered through the woods, keeping a discrete distance from her.

As she idled on the rock, she heard a delicate music weaving its way between the arms of the forest. She got up and followed the sound to a clearing overlooking the waters of Lake Tazia. She waited, wrapped in the integrity of the music. When it stopped, she separated the branches before her and entered the clearing, startling the musician.

"Whose songs are these?" she demanded without introduction.

"They're mine."

"Then I'll have you play more for me."

"I'm sorry, but I can't." James got up from the ground with his guitar in his hand.

"I want to hear your music."

"I'm sorry, but I have to go to work. If I don't start back now, I'll be late." He picked up his knapsack and headed across the clearing.

"Wait. You can't go. Who are you?"

"James McCautry," he answered while walking away from her.

Kate regarded him with offense. She gathered her slender figure to full height and pointed an index finger at his back. "You, James McCautry, stop right now."

The sound of her voice alarmed him. He stopped and made his way back to where she stood. Kate held out her hand to him. "I am Katrine of Yves. I am your queen."

"You're joking," James flatly remarked, taking her hand. His eyes scanned her features. They moved across her auburn hair, silky with its deep, gray highlights. His eyes shifted to her dusty travel garment.

She looked down at her wrinkled dress and smoothed its skirt. "I suppose you've no way to know." She called out, "Jenson, I know you and your men have been following me. Show yourselves to this young man." The dense greenery of the forest parted. Several men emerged from the seclusion of the forest.

"There, now," she said with satisfaction. "Who else, but a queen, travels with so many shadows. Come, play for me." She guided James to sit on the ground of the meadow and placed a comforting hand on his shoulder. "Even if you don't believe me, humor me anyway." She sat down next to him, laying her hands in her lap. As James embraced his guitar and began to play, Kate let the music overcome her. "I've been waiting for this for a long time," she thought, enthralled by the music and his presence.

Katrine's ambition was to organize the arts of her world. It had always been her dream to ensure an untainted environment for artistic genius to flourish. The older, master artists from the years of her father's reign helped Kate initiate her plan while she was still a young girl. They structured the disciplines under the control of the monarchy, establishing Royal Orders for each of the arts. They developed the original guidelines for selecting new artists to enter the Royal Orders. The guidelines were strict, emphasizing creativity, expertise in craft and public appeal. New members of the Royal Orders were taught advanced skills by the master artists. Once an artist became a member of one of the Royal Orders of the arts, social and financial success were guaranteed by the Court.

Under the original system Kate devised, events were scheduled to show the work of the royal artists to the people of Fiara. Free banquets, concerts and shows provided a venue for the artists' talent. In the original system, the work produced by the royal artists could not be bought. The system designed by the master artists was fruitful. Its members produced exceptional artistic works, but it was expensive to operate. As years passed, the treasury funds dwindled under the burden of the Royal Orders and its elite members.

When the master artists aged and entered their twilight years, Kate decided it was time to appoint an advisor from the noblemen at court to help oversee the operation of the Royal Orders. Kate hoped to boost the failing system into a new era of productivity. She chose Sir Henry Caldwell to lead the project. Sir Henry Caldwell controlled a large section of the middle kingdom surrounding the shores of Lake Tazia. Caldwell possessed a searing enthusiasm for the arts and professed an unfailing loyalty to the ideals of the young queen. Fraught with ambitious energy, he accepted the appointment with relish.

During the first year of Caldwell's new assignment, the queen wrestled with personal and political unrest that sprung from her relationship with the Chancellor of Science, Lord Pilchard. The queen found it necessary to focus her energies in calming the political storms brewing and withdrew her influence from the management of the royal orders. Left unchecked in the supervision of the arts, Caldwell began to implement his own ideas. He enlarged the size of the royal orders and expanded the scope of artistic practice. He kept a small schedule of free concerts, balls and artistic shows to maintain a semblance of the original design, while he developed a line of artistic services that could be purchased by a contribution to the monarchy. Convincing the queen that it was necessary to control the quality of the instruments and artistic tools used by artists, Caldwell mandated that all instruments and materials associated with the arts be made and sold only by artisans controlled by the court. Under the Caldwell system, the once depleted treasury swelled and bulged with revenue.

Although the queen did not approve of Caldwell's methods, she exalted in the steady flow of revenue into the treasury. Katrine knew her early vision was financially impossible to bear. She resigned herself to compromise and publicly confirmed Caldwell's control over the royal orders. The next two decades brought a steady decline in the quality of the arts in Fiara. Gifted artists were difficult to find. The court artists relied more and more on established arrangements of older works, predictably acceptable to the people of Fiara. Corruption throughout the royal orders flourished, while immoral and unethical dealings seethed beneath a mask of propriety. The problems were compounded by Grogg. It was a drink that had become entrenched in court rituals, and it seemed at times that there were insufficient quantities to appease the noblemen's insatiable appetite for the brew. Lord Pilchard was the only one who knew how to make it. Grogg was brewed by the Lord Chancellor of Science in the mountains beyond the Epping Wall. It was to those mountains that the queen had banished him. His beverage gave him leverage at court from within the unwilling confinement of his mountain lair.

Pilchard could not be trusted; but as long as he remained in the mountains beyond the Epping Wall, the queen felt safe.

Although she recognized the danger that Pilchard posed, Katrine still remained lenient in her dealings with him. Some said she was soft hearted. Some said she was in love. Over the years, Pilchard took advantage of her gentle attitude, eventually daring to invade the queen's property by encroaching upon a small basin of land within the boundaries of Fiara. The land was rescued by Lord Eastham's forces.

The first moment he heard about the Queen's trials with Lord Pilchard, Lord Eastham rallied his men to fight. Against a ravenous and relentless onslaught, Lord Eastham and his men worked feverishly to push the boundary of Fiara back to its original site of the Epping Wall. Once Pilchard had retreated into the mountains again, Lord Eastham set up a line of defense to thwart future assaults through the Epping Wall. He was awarded additional land for his gallant effort, and he was given a place of honor at the Queen's court.

Although all of the court felt threatened by Pilchard's desire to take land in Fiara, many fervently desired the Grogg he brewed in the sanctuary of the mountains beyond the Epping Wall. They did not want to disrupt the flow of the drink into Fiara. So, they bartered with him and tried to establish a political exception that would permit them to continue to receive his product, while nullifying his claim to dominion. They acknowledged the need for his representative at Court and tolerated the representative he sent to them. He sent Bandore.

Bandore was a man of dubious character. He worked hard, every day that he was allowed into Fiara, to increase the need for Lord Pilchard's product, Grogg. A sinister atmosphere always accompanied his visits. Bandore enjoyed manipulating the people he met by provoking antagonistic situations, hoping he could move them to violence. He played with his victims, until they were caught in a web of deception that left them socially compromised and emotionally weak. They were often left as a target for false accusation and always severely punished by the authorities of the world. Bandore always remained protected by the immunities guaranteed by the Court.

As Pilchard's influence permeated the Court, the decay within the Royal Orders magnified. Kate was forced by her ethics to confront Caldwell's administration. She instructed Sir Henry Caldwell to gather her artistic producers.

"Gentlemen, we have a crisis on our hands. I'll need your help solving it. Beginning today, I will take an active part in the administration of the artistic orders. Sir Henry will assume the role of Advisor. His authority, however, will not diminish. I will work with him to promote a stronger organization with higher quality. I intend to concern myself with assuring the quality of the artistic orders. From this day, no one may be dismissed from the artistic orders without my approval. From this day, only people with exceptional gifts may enter the Royal Artistic Orders, only with my approval. Any requests for performances will be carefully reviewed on an individual basis, especially if the performance has revenue attached to it. And, let the troubadours and local artists handle the balance of the demand for our services."

A cry of protest ran through the group attending the announcement. The Queen could hear snatches of their arguments and demands.

"The troubadours, Your Majesty, are second rate. The people are demanding a higher caliber musical performance than what they are capable of giving."

"They are irresponsible and often incompetent in performing. That is why such a burden has fallen upon the

Royal Order of Musicians. The accounts prove it. We have requests from even simple tavern owners."

"And, the local artists are mere amateurs. You can't expect them to create anything of worth, let alone draw a crowd."

Denton, a thin, ungainly man known for his sharp business sense interrupted them. "Your Majesty, the requests the gentlemen are so valiantly defending comprise a great portion of the income of the Treasury. Losing such a large income presents a financial crisis for Fiara."

"I am aware that we must maintain a reasonable flow of revenue into the Treasury of Fiara. I don't intend to destroy our potential for earning an income. However, it seems to me that the Royal Order of Musicians has been excessively shrewd in its business maneuvers. It has nearly rendered the class of musical troubadours obsolete. I don't believe we need to be greedy within our competitive edge. Do you agree, Sir Henry?"

"I agree, Your Majesty."

"From this moment, no one pays to enter the Royal Artistic Orders." Katrine sternly looked across the sea of faces confronting her.

"Your Majesty," Denton intervened. "I find your directives, as a whole, without flaw. However, I am concerned about several noblemen who have already contributed large amounts to our Treasury in support of their applicants to the artistic orders. They have been assured that their applicants will be accepted into the Royal Orders."

"You will have to disappoint them and return their contributions." Kate's words grated against his calm expression.

"Yes, Your Majesty, I understand. May I bring to your attention one particular contributor, who has shown magnanimous loyalty and unfailing devotion to your government?"

"Lord Windham, Your Majesty," Sir Henry interjected. Katrine winced at the name. She ignored the amusement crossing Sir Henry's face.

"Lord Windham contributed a very large sum of money to the Royal Order of Musicians to secure a place for his granddaughter, Rose. He has an idea that she has astounding musical potential, if given the right environment to develop it. With his contribution came a military and economic pledge for unfailing support for your government by his family." Sir Henry smiled. "Lord Windham is a valuable ally."

"Yes, I know." Kate carefully mulled over his words. It was Lord Windham and Lord Devdon who had protected her when Lord Pilchard and his men threatened to overthrow her reign in Fiara. Without them, she wondered if she would have seen another day of life. Their stature in her court was invincible, even in their twilight years. Their happiness was important to her.

"What instrument does Rose play?"

"None, yet," Denton uneasily replied.

"Well, then, she sings?"

"Some claim she does, but it's too early to tell."

"What do you mean; it's too early to tell?"

Sir Henry smiled and interrupted, "He means that she is young and her voice will change."

"How old, Sir Henry?"

"Five."

"Five?"

"Yes, five." Sir Henry held up his hand illustrating the number.

Kate sourly eyed the congregation before her. "Are there any others?"

"Yes, but none with so delicate a political situation." Sir Henry folded his hands.

Kate exhaled a sigh. "Rose Windham is admitted into the Royal Order of Musicians."

"You have chosen wisely." Sir Henry led the others in a bow. His smile irked Kate.

It took most of her time and effort over the next decade to try to stem the cancerous deterioration of the artistic orders. Even with her sincerest attentions, pockets of corruption sprung into being and grew like an infected sore, contaminating the moral fabric of her government. Many of her directives were sabotaged by the political opposition to undermine her power and authority in the world. Bandore continued promoting Lord Pilchard's product and stirred up trouble with a relentless passion, until Katrine exhausted herself trying to reverse the multiple streams of contention in her government. In a frantic attempt to escape from the many pressures mounting at the Castle Yves, Katrine journeyed into the heart of Fiara, visiting the nobility and common people across her land. After several months of travel, her political power and authority was restored. She was returning to Yves to claim her victory when her coach broke down on the outskirts of Sumatra. She balked at the delay in her schedule. Thinking of her trials, a sigh of relief escaped Kate's lips, and she laughed. James broke melody.

"You don't like it," he said in disappointment.

"Don't be silly. I love it. I haven't heard anything so fresh in a long time. Tell me. What are you doing here?"

"I'm playing at a nearby tavern. I'm a troubadour."

"You're a troubadour?"

"Yes," James began to answer her question, but was overpowered by her peals of laughter. With her amusement, James found himself quite dismayed.

8

Kate invited James to accompany her in her coach on her return to the Castle Yves. She dispatched a messenger to Sumatra for his belongings and directed the messenger to pay his debts. The coach wound its way through the countryside, the route bringing them through key cities in the north. En route, the Queen wove her vision for his musical future. She loved his music. She planned to set him apart from the others in the Music Order. Listening to her stream of words, James was taken by her stately, generous nature, the fluent gestures of her hands, her perceptive sense of humor, the way she patted his knee with motherly touch.

He was like a child anticipating their arrival at the Castle Yves, barely containing his impatience on the long journey. Restless and eager, he entertained the Queen by singing short ditties. He was singing a song for her when a turn in the road allowed him a glimpse of the impressive towers of the castle. He leaned his head out the window of the coach in excitement. "It's really Yves," he called to the Queen.

"Of course, it is. Now bring your head back in."

At her command, James drew his head back inside the coach and picked up the song where he had left off. He vented his thrill in energetic rhythm, mimicking the bumping and jarring of the carriage as it picked up speed in its approach to the castle. As the coach pulled through the castle gates, he stopped playing.

"I have them slow the horses when we get inside the castle grounds," the Queen explained. "They send a messenger to Sir Henry Caldwell as soon as they see my horsemen in the distance. Sir Henry is my Advisor for the Royal Orders. He'll be waiting for me. It never fails."

True to her words, Sir Henry Caldwell and his valet, Chad, awaited their arrival on the verandah of the main courtyard pavement. After the coach halted, a servant opened the door for the Queen. Brushing the servant aside, Sir Henry helped her disembark.

"Good afternoon, Your Majesty. You had a pleasant journey, I hope." Sir Henry guided the queen away from the coach to the steps leading into the castle. He ignored James.

"Interesting would be more accurate to describe our adventure, Sir Henry. All is well here I trust."

Sir Henry glanced uneasily at her as she removed his hand from her arm. "Yes, all is well here. A few matters came up while you were gone, but they can wait until later. We've a banquet and a reception planned to honor your return to Yves. It's only a small affair."

"A banquet and reception sounds delightful. You'll enjoy that, James. Sir Henry, see that James is seated next to me at the banquet. I intend to introduce him to the court this evening. Oh, and find him good quarters in the music building, perhaps a suite overlooking the gardens or the pond—something with a view to inspire him. Do that now while I refresh myself. After I do, you and I will discuss the matters that came up while I was away. I don't want to wait until later."

Sir Henry gaped as the Queen waved to James before leading her entourage into the castle. He turned to James in mild disgust and said, "A musician, eh?"

"Songwriter, too," James offered while flinging his knapsack over his shoulder.

"Huh," Caldwell snorted, huffing away from him and into the castle.

"I suppose that means I'm to show you the way," Caldwell's valet sighed. "Come this way, then. No, we haven't time to get your belongings. Sir Henry will be expecting me soon. We'll have them sent over to you later. Come this way now."

The valet led James through a side door of the building. James scrutinized the dimly lit corridor with increasing disappointment.

"Not very impressive is it? Well, don't worry. These are the servant areas. Tonight's affair will be dripping in splendor. That should suit you fine." The valet paused and opened a door to the outside. His nose tasted the fresh air with relief. He walked James through the gardens and sprawling lawns that wove between the many buildings within the castle compound. When they reached an outer perimeter, the valet flourished a hand dramatically toward a tiered building. It nestled along the gentle slope that followed the shoreline of a pond.

"This is Altmont," the valet explained. "This is where you will live and work." He pointed to one of the many wings that sprouted from the core of the building. "Over there, in that end, are the practice rooms. And over there is a small concert hall. Come with me."

He led James through the front entrance into a lobby. A young man attending the reception desk peered at the newcomer and stiffened his guard. "Who is that one, Chad?"

"He's a new musician."

"I never received orders for a new arrival."

"Well, you have now. Take care of him. I have to be getting back."

"Hold on. We are not supposed to be receiving anymore musicians. It's right here, in the orders from Sir Henry."

"You should know by now that there are always exceptions. This is an exception."

"If I get in trouble, I'll drag you right along beside me."

"I doubt that you will get in trouble," Chad said in a snobbish tone of dismissal and left the building.

"I never know when to obey an order around here," the receptionist grumbled, leering at James. "I guess we have you, like it or not. My name is Jackman." He held out a hand to James.

"James McCautry."

"Well, James. I'll see if I can find you a room in the barracks."

"The Queen suggested a suite overlooking the pond."

"I am sure she did," Jackman laughed. "But a room in the barracks will have to do. I'll see if I can manage a view of the pond, though."

The room was small; its furnishings meager. James could hear music floating through the single window. The only view was an adjacent wing of practice rooms. Dumping his knapsack in a corner, he looked around discouraged. He felt imprisoned and wondered why he had wanted it so much. Uneasy with his feelings, he paced around the room until its confining size drove him outside. Walking along the pond, he passed an expanse of gardens. The area was fragrant with the heady smell of blossoms. He breathed the aroma in slowly, letting the air soothe him and followed a path into the gardens. The lush green of the manicured brush and the delicate beauty of the flowers swallowed his chagrin and quieted his misgivings. The path opened onto a secluded piece of terrain marked by a stone monument. The monument was polished, its curve standing no higher than his waist. Its presentation was humble with an inscription the only interruption in its smooth surface.

James read the inscription. It took several readings before the full impact of the words hit him. His upper body trembled a little. Even as he tried to check his emotion, tears welled in his eyes. He fondly ran his fingers over the stone, feeling the depth of incision for each letter. As he did, he gently said, "Hello, Neppam. I've been meaning to come see you for the longest time."

"Ho there. You knew Neppam now, did you?"

Cocking an eyebrow with irritation, James wretched from his feelings and turned towards the exuberant voice. His defensiveness was greeted by the cheerful face of a stout, gray-haired gentleman. The joy in his face conquered James. Allowing his shoulders to slump, James nodded.

"Well, so did I!" The man, animated, advanced in friendship. He shook James's hand vigorously. "We were the closest of friends, inseparable, almost. That is until he insisted on moving to that little village on the edge of nowhere. Well, whatever made him happy, that's what I say. Tell me, are you visiting the court? I don't remember seeing you here before."

"I have entered the Royal Order of Musicians. I arrived today, Sir."

"You are a musician! Oh, good. I don't know many of you, and we have something in common. Knowing Neppam, I mean. And you knew him from where?"

"My village in Poule. I grew up in Poule where he lived."

"Yes, that's the name of the place. Huh. He liked it there. He really liked it there. It must have been a treat seeing

Neppam as you grew up. He started wearing robes back then—silly robes—not exactly normal clothing for Fiara. I couldn't tell him a thing, though. He wouldn't listen to any of us. He had his own ideas, his own ways. I suppose, it would have been a shame to change him. I, for one, liked him just as he was."

His cheerful manner wavered for a moment. He struggled to recapture his mood. "So you knew my dear, dear friend. What luck! We'll have to talk, you and I. The first moment I have a chance. Right now, I am late. I am in the middle of hubbub about a reception for the queen, as if we don't have enough receptions around here. I am on committee again, but I needed to catch my breath for a moment. When I need quiet, I come here. I always come here. I am sure we will meet again soon," he said reaching for James's hand before leaving. "My name is Pembroke, for future reference." With an excited grin, the man hurried down the path, quickly disappearing from view.

James sat on the lawn in front of the monument. His emotions flailed him. It seemed Neppam was waiting for him all along. Somehow, it seemed right. He watched the light cross the stone and deepen into shadows announcing the approach of evening. When he felt the brisk tickling of early evening over his arms, he got up and walked back to his room in Altmont. A change of clothes, crisp and new, lay neatly on his bed. A travel bag with the clothing he accumulated in Sumatra hugged against the bureau. His guitar balanced against the wall next to the window.

Jackman knocked once before letting himself into the room. "You are to attend the Queen's banquet. There's a reception afterwards. Chad sent over some clothes for you to wear. He said he doubted you had anything suitable for the occasion. You can bathe down the hall. I'll take you there. Oh, and Chad said you are to shave. You don't look like you need it tonight, but you'll have to shave anyways."

James finished dressing as Chad arrived to escort him to the main building of the castle for the banquet. A crowd was milling about the hall, leisurely chatting. The Queen was to meet him there. A fanfare of trumpets and drums would signal their entrance into the banquet hall.

"Why can't we walk in with everyone else?" James wanted to know.

"Oh no, that's impossible. You've got to make a grand entrance. That's what impresses them."

"Well, I'll feel pretty foolish."

"Probably, but you'll get used to it soon enough."

James sat down in an oversized chair in resignation. He watched Chad snap last minute orders to the army of servants scuttling the banquet hall. As the hall began to fill with guests, Chad retreated to the vestibule with James. "There. I think everything is ready." He drew the curtains, enclosing them in privacy. "Almost everyone is here now. We just have to wait for the Queen."

"Am I supposed to play tonight?" James inquired. "No one has said for sure."

"No, you don't have to play tonight. This one is just for show."

When the Queen arrived, James took his place at her side. On Chad's cue, the sound of a drum resounded throughout the hall. The Court trumpeters heralded their instruments. The curtains opened. The Queen and James entered under the hushed reverence of the crowd. James felt foolish; but he graciously hid his discomfort, accompanying the Queen with the finesse of a nobleman. They took their places at the head table, standing while Caldwell welcomed the Queen home from her travels. After Caldwell finished, the Queen introduced James to the Court members. She extolled his musical gift and promised he would perform for the Court at a future date.

As the Queen finished speaking and a toast was initiated, James's eyes were drawn to a man at a nearby table. The man stood with the others at the onset of the toast, lifted his glass, bowed to James and pointed to his own rear end. James almost choked on his wine as he recognized that the man was his friend, John. John bowed again, flicking the underside of his nose at James to signify a snob. His point made, he sat down disgruntled. Fortunately for John, his antics were witnessed only by a few members of the nobility. The Queen missed the entire episode.

9

The days following the Queen's banquet were filled with introductory meetings with various members of the musical court. During his first meeting with Sir Henry Caldwell, James requested that Caldwell pair him with his former partner, John. Caldwell resisted the match.

"It's enough we have two with your background," Caldwell said, furrowing his brow and rubbing his chin. "You'll both need a refining influence to mold you an acceptable public image. No, John stays with Boyden's group. They play well together and have developed a good rapport with each other."

"But, John and I have played together for years. We have an excellent rapport. Some of my best work has been with him."

"That may be true," Caldwell folded his hands on the table before him. "I still feel both of you would benefit from the separation."

"I think you are wrong. No, I know it."

"It doesn't matter what you think. My decision is final. As for you, I haven't decided yet. You'll study under Denton's supervision for the time being. He'll assign your rehearsal schedule and keep track of your progress. We'll meet again when I come to a decision about your future."

When James returned to the music barracks after his meeting with Caldwell, John greeted him, eager for news of the outcome.

"You're staying with Boyden. He's isolating me."

"Great. You overcame him with your charm." John flopped onto the bed with his words.

"Get off. I want to lie down." James prodded him until he moved off the bed.

"I'm your guest. You take the floor."

"I am not in the mood, John."

"Look. Don't worry. Caldwell is just pulling rank on us. He is letting everyone know he is still in charge, in spite of the fact that the Queen has made a fuss over you. He'll let us play together when it is his idea. You understand?"

James opened a window, trying to hide his feelings of dejection. "I have a feeling Caldwell wants to make me suffer in my good fortune."

"You're probably right. But, as long as you come out ahead in the end, why should you care?"

"I care." He dug his hand along the windowsill.

"Don't ever let him know it."

James heaved a sigh. Sliding to the floor, he let his head rest against the wall. As he closed his eyes, tension built along his forehead. A knock on the door interrupted the silence. Boyden let himself into the room.

"It didn't go well," Boyden surmised. "I guess that means John is still playing with us."

"He's still with you."

"All right, we rehearse again in an hour." Boyden turned to James. "What about you?"

"Denton's supervising me. I'm not assigned to any group."

"I expected as much. I wish he had assigned you to me. I suggested it. I also recommended that you and John work together. It seems a shame to split up a good musical team, but Caldwell has final say around here. You better try to get on his good side."

"Thanks for trying, Boyden." John reached out to him and shook his hand firmly.

"Rehearsal in an hour," Boyden reminded him and left the room.

In the evening, they met James for dinner. John contemplated James throughout the meal, assessing the discouragement that seemed to ebb underneath his friendly discourse. During a lull in the conversation, John offered a suggestion.

"We can still play music together, James, if we work around our schedules. We don't need Caldwell's approval for that, do we, Boyden?"

"As long as you follow your assigned schedules, no one should have any reason for objection." Boyden glanced at the two men. "Of course, Sir Henry will feel like you are trying to openly defy him, but I don't think he will interfere."

"Good, then we will play together in the evenings. You and Eric are always welcome at our rehearsals. You can play with us, if you like. We need a fuller sound to really perform our music the way we envision it."

"I'll help you in any way that I can," Boyden assured him.

The next day, James began his grueling sessions under Denton. James labored with the discipline required to meet Denton's expectations. As each day passed, it became more difficult for him to concentrate. His waning focus inflamed animosity in his musical supervisor. Denton increased his technical demands on James and structured the day even more strictly. James suffocated under the creative restraints. The wear on his nerves depleted his physical energy. By the end of each day, he fell exhausted onto his bed. In the latter part of the evenings, he rehearsed with John.

When the demands upon him reached unbearable proportions, James would lock his door and lay himself down in his bed with the crystal wing around his neck. There, in the semidarkness, he would soar once again to the jewel on the mountain submerging his aching soul in its soothing light. He never was able to move past the steep meadow lands to the land beyond the stark wall. He tried and tried; but each time he willed himself beyond it, he was pulled back into the dreary reality of his new life. Even so, each time he returned to his room, he felt he returned with an intangible gain. The more he used the crystal wing, the more difficult it was for him to imagine his life without it.

Several weeks after the Queen's reception, James received an invitation to visit the main quarters of the castle. When the invitation arrived, he was playing music with John and Boyden in one of the Altmont practice rooms.

"Can't you get out of it tonight?" John fussed over the interruption in their work. "We're in the middle of this and we don't get much time to work on it."

"No, I have to go. It bears the royal seal. He must be one of the queen's advisors."

"Who is it from?" Boyden's curiosity was teaming.

James handed him the note. "Lord William Pembroke. I met him when I first arrived here at the castle."

"Oh, it's only Willie," Boyden laughed returning the note to James. "Tell him you are busy. He won't mind. Honest. He'll ask you to meet with him another time."

"No. I'm going." James felt loyalty for Lord Pembroke rising swiftly within him. He placed his instrument to the side and left the practice room.

Lord Pembroke stood in an upper story window looking across the gardens in the direction of Altmont. He barely made out the shadowy figure moving through the twilight across the lawns to the main quarters. When he identified James, he called a servant to prepare tea. The knock on the door echoed through the chamber. Pembroke hurried to answer the door himself. He offered an apology to his servant as he waved him into another room, then opened the door for James.

Lord Pembroke welcomed James with a heartfelt hug and swept him into the library on a stream of words. Pembroke sat behind his desk, offering James a seat next to him. Without waiting for James to seat himself, Pembroke expounded his pleasure with their chance meeting in the gardens. He continued on a whirlwind of words and joyful exuberance, expressing his hope for James's successful transition into his new life within the Royal Orders.

"Tell me," Lord Pembroke folded his hands with concern, "is it going well here?"

James avoided contact with Pembroke's eyes. "Yes, it's going well."

"You seem hesitant. It bothers me. Aren't you happy?"

"I suppose I am. I always wanted this. It's just very different from what I imagined." James leaned an elbow against the arm of the chair, resting his chin in his hand.

"In what way is it different?" Pembroke's round face appealed to him with the tenderness of a father.

"Oh, I don't know. Everything is so structured here. I'm used to having a say in my life." James hesitated, searching his feelings before speaking. "I guess I'm disappointed because they've separated me from my partner. We have played music together for a very long time. I have written songs with him. Good ones. We have our own sound. We always dreamed and worked for this, but we always planned on staying together when we joined the royal orders. It hasn't worked out the way we planned. Caldwell thinks we'll do better separated. I am doing drills with Denton." James rolled his eyes. "If you ever did drills with Denton, you'd understand why I am unhappy."

"Is that all that is troubling you! You don't like working with Denton and you want to work with your partner? I will take care of that for you right away. What is your partner's name?"

"John Yates."

"All right, that is easy enough to fix. Consider it done. I will speak to the Queen myself about it. It won't do to have you unhappy." Using the desktop, Pembroke pushed himself to a standing position. He sat on a corner of the desk enjoying the amazement crossing James's face. "So, you are the little boy from Poule. Neppam wrote to me about you. He never mentioned your name. He said he knew a boy who was extremely gifted in music. It was fated that you would eventually get here, as good as Neppam felt you were." The broad smile on his face waned. "You didn't know he was dead, did you? I could tell by the look on your face."

"I haven't been back to Poule in years. I didn't expect to find him here."

"Oh, he isn't here. It is just a monument. He was buried in Poule. They couldn't take him here. It was too far away. It was much too far away." Pembroke lowered his head in respect for his old friend.

"I didn't know he had friends at Court." James pensively looked as if searching the air for memories of the past.

"I know you didn't. I bet you didn't know much about him at all. That is just like him. That is just like him." Pembroke chuckled, and then turned on a more serious note. "Oh, he had his own ways. That is for sure. Secretive. He insisted on secret. Well, there is no reason now to keep anything under our hats. I, at least, have the pleasure of telling you all about him." Pembroke leaned back twiddling his fingers as he reflected. "Now, what do I tell you?" He mused, before turning and addressing him in a strong, sure voice. "Lord David Neppam Devdon was his full title. Only his closest friends called him Neppam. He was a noble man from a family of reputable origin in Fiara. He was the Lord Protector of Yves. You are probably familiar with the title. That was Neppam. Yes, he was a valuable man here at court. Then, he got it into his head he wanted no more of it. Not a thing. Traded it all in for a quiet corner on the edge of nowhere. Neppam's life in Poule must have been quite different from all of this." Pembroke opened his arms as if to introduce the grandeur of the surroundings with his gesture.

"Neppam liked it in Poule," James reminded him.

"Yes, isn't that just like him? Well, I guess he tired of all of this. He could have had everything. He wanted nothing. Can you imagine that! It never was the same after he left." A wistful look crossed Pembroke's face.

"So, you built a monument for him."

"Not me. The Queen did it. Oh, I did suggest that we do a likeness of him. I was thinking of something dynamic, like him in battle. Young, virile, the way he used to be. The Queen liked him the way he was, old. I would never have suggested a likeness if I thought they would have him old. So, we settled on the stone, humble. It suited him better."

"I don't ever remember him young," James said with softness in every part of his tone.

"Of course, you wouldn't remember him young." Pembroke reached over and petted his hand in sympathy. "I suppose old does well for you. You didn't know him at any other time of his life. I remember him young, vibrant, courageously battling Pilchard." Pembroke jabbed the air around him, excitedly punctuating each memory with energy.

"Neppam fought Pilchard?"

"Yes, he did. You don't reach Neppam's status at Court without doing something extraordinary. We are all of good ancestry here, except for a few of the artists. Neppam fought Pilchard. Lord Protector of Yves. That is what it means. You have heard of the title, at least. Oh, those were exciting days at

Yves. I was very young back then and much younger than Neppam. I looked up to him. He was such a dynamic figure and favored by the Court. Well, rumor had it that the King had him on his list for Katrine's hand in marriage. The word was that he turned the King down in his offer. They say he told him that the choice for a husband for Katrine was Katrine's choice to make. He was lucky the King took it as good humor."

Pembroke shook his head a little and chuckled at his thoughts. "The Queen is an attractive woman now for her age, but back then, oh back then, we all had our dreams that she would set her heart on one of us. She had looks, charm, intelligence and the throne of Fiara. She was a good catch without a doubt. She came close to choosing a husband several times; but there was Pilchard always lurking somewhere in the background. He is a scary one. She never did make up her mind. No, she never really made up her mind about that one."

"I don't understand." James leaned forward in interest. "What did Pilchard have to do with the Queen deciding not to marry?"

"Pilchard," Pembroke gave James a knowing glance, "why, he was the Queen's lover, of course."

10

Simeon Pilchard was the stepson of a wealthy nobleman. His stepfather was a trusted advisor and companion of the king. When it was discovered that Simeon had an unusual affinity for alchemy, the king undertook the responsibility of Simeon's education. Simeon was given permanent rooms within the Castle Yves. He grew up in the auspices of the royal family and was treated as one of them. He was taught the well-kept secrets of the art of alchemy by the king's finest alchemists. Very few restrictions were placed on Simeon.

As children, Simeon and the Princess Katrine were constant companions. They bonded early in life, developing a lasting affection for one another. Katrine found Simeon's sullen moods attractive. She accepted him as he was. Her fond tolerance of all aspects of his personality provided Simeon with a pleasant refuge from the harsh jeering of his peers, who felt that his dark and often explosive nature was difficult to accept. As the years passed, he discovered she was the only one with whom he could express his deepest thoughts, great despair and longings in his heart.

The king encouraged the friendship between Simeon and his daughter. Simeon needed someone to trust, if he were to develop into a useful member of the court, and Katrine needed Simeon. Simeon was loyal to her and sensitive to her every need. She found great joy in his company. As they grew older, the king noticed that their love went beyond mere friendship. He began to worry that their love could not be contained within the cultural protocols of Fiara. The king subtly began to divert Katrine's attention away from Simeon.

Katrine held a strong concern for the arts. Knowing her deep commitment and love of artistic culture, the king created a position within his government for Katrine to implement her ideas and taste the responsibility she one day would inherit from him. Her young mind ignited with the opportunity given her. She gave birth to a compelling vision of an organized structure for the arts in which the quality of work could be controlled through the monarchy. When her father gave her permission to pursue her ideas further, she buried herself in the initial phases of her plan. Her studies and her work left her little time to spend with Simeon. Kate managed to maintain their relationship anyway, deepening their bonds.

Simeon's love bloomed for Kate. He fought its relentless, drawing, physical force until he found the courage to approach her father and request her hand in marriage. When he did, his romantic hopes were destroyed in swift, cold words sending him into a cruel emotional tailspin. The king reminded Simeon that he never would hold title or land, according to the laws of Fiara. Since Simeon's stepfather had no direct heir, the titles and land would fall into the possession of the monarchy. Without title, Simeon would never be considered an appropriate match for the successor to the throne.

In spite of Katrine's pleading, the king refused to change the law and break the entrenched tradition of their society. He contracted the betrothal of his daughter to Lord Weldon of Ashby-Oane, a handsome young nobleman of considerable wealth and political stature. Once she was betrothed, Katrine's contact with Simeon was restricted. Lord Weldon was a pleasant and kind man. His good looks and appealing charm made it difficult for Kate to enforce an attitude of cool distance or rejection. They soon became a close pair. Simeon could not accept the injustice.

It was the first time Simeon experienced the fiery cavern of hate and discontent. It smothered him in its darkness. It lodged itself in every fiber of his being. He vehemently protested to the king, determined to change the king's mind. Sensing Simeon's growing rage, the king dispatched Simeon to Eastham for study with the retired master of alchemy, Darmon. Simeon loathed the idea of leaving Katrine. He beseeched her to stand firm in his absence from the castle and not marry the Lord of Ashby-Oane.

The alchemist, Darmon, resided in seclusion on the eastern shore of Lake Knapp in South Eastham. Supplies were transported to him from the court on a regular schedule. The bleak solitude of the area suited Darmon's surly disposition. Darmon avoided contact with his fellow man as much as possible. His craggy and pessimistic character prevented success in his relationships with other people. Darmon's cold, disgruntled attitude fed Simeon's own incubating gloom. The two rarely spoke with each other, unless the subject pertained to his studies.

Within his forlorn existence, Simeon discovered relief in exploring the countryside south of Darmon's abode. Along the southern shoreline of Lake Knapp, a wall of smooth cliffs rose to staggering heights above the water. The cliffs were an extension of the Epping Wall, a natural barrier to the deserted caverns and marshlands of the southeastern corner of the world. The only entrance through the stone wall was a small pass large enough for a single horseman to navigate the rocky terrain.

Pilchard was intrigued by the land beyond the wall. It was several months before he could take time to guide his steed through the narrow, treacherous passage into the mountains. When he did, he discovered a dismal land. The mountain bases were seeped in a wet marshland, leading into the thick bogs of Fiara. A fog hugged the base of the mountain range. The steep, angular slopes of the mountains lay barren of vegetation, passable only by foot.

Pilchard tethered his horse in the rocks along the entrance to the mountains. Alone, he walked the arid turf, investigating the jagged mountainsides. After months of intermittent, persistent searching, he uncovered an opening to the black interior of the mountains. The mountains disguised a system of caverns extending for miles within the bowels of the region.

Using torches fashioned in Darmon's laboratory, Simeon explored the expansive tunnels and stone chambers of the underworld. He wandered for hours in the sanctum of its cheerless surroundings. He derived a mysterious pleasure from its narrow passageways of damp rock, the vacuous chambers of hardened silence, and the inner streams carving its scourged, hidden face.

When the meager light from his torches diminished, he ventured to the surface again. Outside, he roamed the marshlands, visually sifting through its stark reeds and indistinct flora. A vivid flower on spindly stalk grew in abundance amid the dull colors of the wet slue. Its bright petals pierced the drab landscape—a fresh promise from within the murky swamp. Simeon, entranced by the simple beauty of the flower, gathered sample bunches for his studies. In the laboratory, Simeon dissected the exquisite petals and juicy leaves of the plant he named Semola. Using Darmon's inventive techniques, he secretly experimented with the plant hoping to one day refine its sweet nectar into a potent brew.

Months passed without word from the Castle Yves. Separated from the outside world, Simeon consoled himself with his excursions beyond the Epping Wall and his stringent experiments with the Semola plant. At the end of a year, the king sent orders for Simeon to continue his studies as an apprentice to Darmon. Several months later, Darmon received a message from the castle. The king had passed away. Simeon was called to the castle for a period of mourning. Excited, anticipating his reunion with Katrine, Simeon rode without rest, until he entered the gates at Yves.

At Yves, Katrine shied away from Simeon's unguarded familiarity. She was distant and formal in their encounters, avoiding any suggestion of intimacy between them. Simeon repressed his anger, attending the funeral for the king without showing his disdain at the presence of the Lord of Ashby-Oane at Kate's side. For weeks after the funeral, Simeon pressed Katrine to meet with him. His requests were refused.

Simeon remained a ward of the crown until after the coronation. After Katrine assumed her throne, Simeon was granted an audience with the Queen to decide his status with the monarchy. At the audience, the Queen renewed the court commitment to Simeon's education. She ordered him to continue his apprenticeship with Darmon. Wretched with disappointment, Simeon prepared for his return to Lake Knapp.

Late in the evening, before his departure, Katrine stole into his rooms. At the sight of her clad in the soft white ruffles of her evening wear, Simeon's stiff heart warmed. He pulled her into a welcome embrace, holding her near as he listened to her defense. Many members of the court supported her father's contract with Lord Weldon of Ashby-Oane. They opposed her association with him. Simeon would have to be patient until she could secure her authority as monarch of the world. He was to return to Lake Knapp and Darmon. When Darmon confirmed his mastery of the art of alchemy, Katrine would call him to Yves and appoint him Lord Chancellor of Science. With the title, he would be awarded land and a permanent position with the court. As she spoke with him, he nestled close to her, his long checked passion overcoming her. The next day, with Kate's sweet breath still pulsing in his ear, Simeon left Yves appeased.

With increasing concern, Simeon lived and worked as Darmon's apprentice. Each time the wagons arrived with supplies, Simeon impatiently interrogated the drivers for news from the castle. From them, he learned Katrine had organized the arts. Banquets, festivals and theatrical shows were entertaining the people throughout Fiara. Royal Musicians toured the world on a regular schedule. The people were content with Kate's rule. They trusted her and supported her vision for their world. As Kate's authority grew stronger, Simeon waited for news that she had rejected Lord Weldon of Ashby-Oane. When it did not come, he found himself traveling the land beyond the Epping Wall more and more.

After two long years, Darmon sent a letter to the Queen verifying Simeon's mastery of alchemy. Simeon was summoned by the Queen to assume his post of Lord Chancellor of Science. Upon arriving at Yves, Simeon was pressured by the attending nobility to maintain a respectable distance from Katrine. He adhered to their warnings only in public, holding a constant rendezvous with her in secret. His love affair with the Queen did not go unnoticed by the nobility for long. Their clandestine meetings, under the cover of night, eventually spilled into the daylight hours. Kate invented reasons to consult with Simeon. Her longing for him deepened, flowing freely from her eyes whenever they met in his official capacity of Lord Chancellor of Science.

Spurred by Lord Weldon of Ashby-Oane, dissension among the nobility built to a dangerous level against the Queen and her liaisons with Pilchard. Even Lord David Neppam Devdon found it difficult to sway the growing unrest against the Queen. Recognizing the peril she faced in neglecting her legal responsibility to Lord Weldon, Lord Devdon persuaded Katrine to restrain her affair with Simeon.

Feeling spurned once again, Simeon yielded his peace of mind with Kate's decision to pacify the noblemen of the court. Degraded by her rejection, he embedded himself in his work, his anger simmering in hot waves beneath his congenial front. When Kate first noticed his evolving scorn, she tried to smooth his feelings of offense by offering him a gift. She gave Simeon liberty to introduce his Semola brew to the court as a private business venture. It was a heavy statement of her allegiance to him. With the support of the queen, the delectable flavor of the brew was hungrily received by the court. It rapidly became the drink of choice even among the noblemen who with vicious arrogance often tormented him. The popularity of the brew overflowed onto Simeon, elevating his social standing within the community at Yves and increasing his personal fortune.

Pleased with the glory of his newfound notoriety, Simeon continued his research into the hidden wonders of the Semola plant. With energetic diligence, fired by court encouragement, he soon discovered that a minor deviation in the formula altered the effects of his brew in an insidious way. Simeon dubbed the new Semola brew Grogg. The name tickled his black sense of humor. He launched the new formula with its subtle character into the court without informing the Queen. Wisely, he kept his perfected Semola formula to himself, supplying the court with batches he brewed within the mountain caverns beyond the Epping Wall. His strict authority over his product increased its value. The court members quickly incorporated it among their daily rituals without realizing its pervasion over their will.

The ever increasing presence of Lord Pilchard within the scheme of court politics concerned Lord Devdon. Pilchard had gathered an unseemly group of followers from outside the nobility. The men serving him were of despicable character and their presence on the castle grounds disturbed Devdon. Rumors citing growing numbers of Pilchard followers from among the rabble of Fiara troubled him even more. Pilchard's own growing ignoble mannerisms disrupted the calm venue of genteel castle life. Pilchard's harsh, unbending resentment toward Kate reflected in his eyes every time chance drew her near him in the course of the days he spent at Yves. As the months wore on, an ominous atmosphere fell over the castle. Kate, enthralled with the heat from her passion, did not notice the changes in Simeon. Lord Devdon did.

A vise of uneasiness gripped Lord Devdon. He began closely watching Pilchard's movements both inside and outside of the castle walls. Among an array of underhanded dealings usurping profit from the treasury, Devdon discovered Pilchard was slowly buying cooperation from the military. Convinced of his desire for vengeance against the Queen, Lord Devdon exposed Pilchard's treachery. Sorrowed, but unconvinced by the evidence against Simeon, the Queen removed herself from his judgment, leaving Simeon at the mercy of Lord Devdon, who was placed in charge of his trial and sentencing.

With Grogg as the sod for their bond, Pilchard boasted friends even among the elite of the nobility. They were adept at defending him against the body of evidence Devdon revealed during the trial. Even so, the testimony from several officers in the military, who were known for their upright character, dealt a fatal blow to the skillful defense presented for Pilchard. It seemed apparent from the testimonies that Pilchard had purchased arms and military cooperation using subversive tactics aimed against the Queen. Although a planned rebellion was never proved, the evidence was enough by the legal standards in Fiara to encourage a severe penalty.

The panel of noblemen reviewing Pilchard's case was split on the type of sentence to invoke. They deliberated at length on an appropriate sentence for the circumstances. His long-standing service to the monarchy, the court investment in his education, his value as a master alchemist, his possession of the Semola formula and the Queen's conviction of his innocence were all factors considered. In the end, a vote was held, and Pilchard was sentenced to death.

The Queen was livid with the decision. She refused to invoke the sentence. Her anger and frustration stormed for weeks, ignescent with the slightest hint of Pilchard's fate. No one dared approach her, except Lord Devdon. Devdon nursed the Queen through the agony and torture of her burden. His patience and kindness soothed her torrid emotions. With his gentle care, Kate accepted the finality of her shattered relationship with Simeon and began to understand the serious threat he posed. She still could not bring herself to sign the order for his death.

As Simeon waited in his cell for his sentence to be carried out, his angry resolve against Katrine deepened. During the weeks of her indecision, his own fear burned the remainder of his love into a cold heartedness. He managed enough contact in the prison to send orders to his men in the military, as well as those outside the castle walls. With strategic finesse his men overran the castle compound and released Simeon from his cell. While Pilchard made his escape, a group of his men attacked the main building where Katrine slept. They dragged her from her bed, intentionally battering her as they struggled to rip her bedclothes from her body. Before they could overcome her, Lord Devdon and his men were aroused. They charged in valiant defense forcing the men to flee. They were strengthened by Lord Windham and Lord Weldon of Ashby-Oane as they gathered the available militia and led them into battle against Pilchard and his men.

Devdon, Windham and Weldon forced Pilchard and his men from Yves into the countryside beyond the castle. While Devdon and Windham secured the castle, Lord Weldon and a group of his men followed the scattering enemy in hot pursuit of Pilchard. Several miles from the castle, Weldon's men were surprised by another attack from a number of Pilchard's men laying in wait in the thickets beyond the line of defense guarding the castle entrance. The men fought with a vicious energy. Weldon's men pulled back towards the castle, their count dwindling. As they neared Yves, Devdon's men reinforced them. Once again, Pilchard's men scattered.

Devdon ordered the Queen's forces to regroup. Parties of men were selected to separate the dead from the wounded. They scuttled the landscape examining their marks. They called as they recognized bodies, their mournful voices echoing across the twilight. Devdon listened with silent compassion to their forlorn wail. He shook his head with regret recognizing the fallen and ordered his men to look for Lord Weldon of Ashby-Oane. There was no need. Lord Weldon was dead.

Before morning broke, Devdon and the militia began the search for Pilchard, following their trail into Eastham. In Eastham, Lord Windham caught up to him with reinforcements. Wary of another surprise attack, Devdon kept their forces together, slowing progress in the search. The Queen's men tracked Pilchard through the diverse terrain in Eastham. Within the forests of Lake Knapp, Pilchard's men struck them with bloody vengeance, defending the turf approaching the open basin along the Epping Wall. While his men diverted the Queen's army, Pilchard slipped across the basin and through the narrow pass, finding refuge in the bleak mountains beyond the Epping Wall. When they felt sure Pilchard was safe, his men dispersed within the thick of the forest. Devdon's army was forced to separate into small units to follow the many trails leading around the lake. By the time the Queen's men tracked them, they were safely through the pass.

As Lord Devdon examined the Eastham side of the narrow pass, he realized that storming the natural fortress formed by the Epping Wall was futile. One by one his men would be slaughtered as they came through the pass to the other side of the Epping Wall. The pass gave Pilchard a military advantage. Lord Devdon knew it also gave the Queen an advantage. He suspected the land beyond the wall was unable to support life for long. Without assistance from the outside world, any supplies Pilchard had stored would eventually deplete. Pilchard and his men would have to surrender or die within the confines of their natural lair. Lord Devdon stationed troops along the basin guarding the pass against Pilchard's escape into Eastham. There, he waited for the inevitable.

After several months, Lord Devdon returned to Yves, turning over his command of the siege to Lord Eastham. At Yves, Devdon was faced with the Queen's weakened resolution to defeat Pilchard. She believed he was right to stand in stubborn defiance of what she deemed an unfair sentence. She couldn't bear the cruelty her army was inflicting upon him. The image of her lover slowly starving to death haunted her. She restlessly walked the castle hallways and grounds, wringing her hands until they bruised. With each passing day, her compassion for his suffering grew stronger and tore deeply within her heart.

Devdon suffered in empathy with the Queen. He knew Pilchard was too dangerous to pardon, but the sight of Kate's agony prompted him to devise a compromise that would satisfy the many factions within the court. Instead of signing an order for his death, Katrine banished Lord Pilchard to the land beyond the Epping Wall. If he crossed the boundary of the Epping Wall, the penalty was death. As a banished citizen of Fiara, Pilchard was free to receive a minimum amount of supplies for his sustenance. Under Kate's direction, a schedule of delivery was immediately instituted to relieve his harried condition. Forces from the noble family of Eastham were commissioned to guard the Epping Wall to ensure Pilchard and his men never came through the pass again. Katrine and her rule appeared safe.

From within his confinement, Pilchard re-establisheded his connections to the court and negotiated trade privileges with the court members for his Semola drink. Using his supply of Grogg to bribe officials, Pilchard bought himself excursions throughout Fiara without the Queen's knowledge. Though risky, his secret journeys throughout the land brought him valuable contacts—contacts he hoped would one day help free him from his mountain prison and establish him as the ruler of Fiara. The means to accomplish his plan in full, however, eluded him, while the real freedom he longed for remained buried with his deadened love for the Queen.

On one of his journeys across the countryside, Pilchard dared travel to a remote section of mountains near the Arca V'ing Enta. There in an isolated village hugging a mountainside, he heard the enchanting verses of an unusual story about a crystal wing that had long ago soared from within the lights of the Arca V'ing Enta. The storyteller claimed the story was true and a man in Fiara now carried the crystal wing. The crystal wing, he said, had power—a power to make men succeed and a power to set men free.

> "With the wings of a bird,
> Ye shall soar to the heights
> And no one shall ever see,

How the wings filled with light,
Brought you power and might
And a way to set you free."

From the moment he heard the verse of promise, Pilchard believed the crystal wing was real. It cemented his hope of one day returning from beyond the Epping Wall to rule Fiara. He and his men searched the world for the man and the crystal wing, but the man was never found.

11

William Pembroke had served the court for many years. Through longevity and persistence, Pembroke rose to the Queen's Counsel. He was a friendly old gentleman who took great pleasure in thoughtful, exuberant conversation. His vibrant enthusiasm spilled over into all facets of court life. Pembroke liked to have his fingers in a little bit of everything. He was involved with every new project crossing the counsel desk—not always successfully. Even as a young man, everything he attempted came out just a little bit wrong.

The Queen was indulgent with Pembroke. His bumbling charm provided light diversion in matters that otherwise would have been dull, bogged down in seriousness and formality. Pembroke was never deterred by his failures. He approached each new project with renewed optimism and vigor. The Queen respected his perseverance against his own flaws. She valued his honest, straightforward opinions on delicate subjects, prized his warm heart, and trusted Pembroke above all others on her Counsel.

When Pembroke informed the Queen that James was unhappy, she immediately set out to correct the problem. The assignment to Denton was cancelled. The Queen directed James and John to join forces as they saw fit. Boyden was instructed to act as mentor for their initial projects. Caldwell was reprimanded for his inappropriate use of talent. Caldwell did not take the chastisement well. His antagonism toward James overflowed in a fountain of resistance each time they encountered each other in the business of the Royal Orders.

With Lord Pembroke and the Queen as his allies, James ignored Caldwell's arrogance. He and John began auditioning musicians for their own musical group. The basic group was composed of a bass player, a pianist, a percussionist and their own guitars. The four instruments provided the fundamental sound and tone. Other musicians were selected to play accompaniments as needed for each arrangement of music. All the musical arrangements were composed by James and John. Boyden assisted with technical orchestration. The arrangements ranged from simple to full sounds. They freely used instruments as their creative impulses urged them, using unusual combinations of instruments to create mood or to stir the soul of the listener. Their simple and unrestrained approach to orchestration yielded a unique sound. Boyden heralded their technique as genius. Caldwell groaned at it.

"What is this sound?" Caldwell lamented when challenging their work early in its first phase. "They've used guitars and a few other instruments thrown in without musical reason. This is what happens when troubadours are allowed entry into the Royal Order of Musicians. They have a natural feel for writing a song, but they haven't the musical training essential to carry out its mission. Their work is primitive."

"Has anyone heard their music yet?" The Queen looked at Caldwell for an answer.

"They are secretive. They ask that we wait until they decide that the music is ready to be heard." Caldwell pouted, disappointed with his exclusion from the project. "I have seen some of the scores. They are sparse with unusual timings for some of the music. It uses heated rhythms with very little formal orchestration. When they use orchestration, it's not what you would expect. I would say they are breaking all the rules, with our permission, of course."

The Queen thoughtfully digested Sir Henry's perspective. She turned to Lord Pembroke. "You like it, Willie?"

"Oh, yes, very much. I think you should hear it for yourself."

Lord Pembroke suggested the Queen visit Altmont and listen to a rehearsal without James and John knowing of her presence in the building. In this way, Pembroke reminded her she could respect their musical privacy and make a reasonable decision regarding their future with the artistic orders. The Queen agreed. The next day, she dressed in common garb and walked to Altmont accompanied only by Lord Pembroke. Caldwell met them discretely at a side door of the building. He opened the door to let them into the building and escorted them into the back of the concert hall. The Queen and Caldwell hid in a cloak room inside the entranceway to the concert hall, while Pembroke diverted James's attention. James waved to his friend when he took a seat in the back row of the hall. Boyden turned and said, "You won't see much from back there."

"Oh, I know." Pembroke chuckled. "I only want to listen today. Will you play the one I heard yesterday, James? You know the one that makes me want to jump around. And that pretty one with all the strings and horns."

"Coming up next," James smiled fondly with Pembroke's requests and signaled the musicians to take up their instruments.

Lord Pembroke settled into his chair delighted with the sound of the music filling the concert hall. As the rehearsal progressed, Lord Pembroke suggested, "Could you do a few songs uninterrupted? The ones I mentioned and perhaps you would do them as if you were performing in a concert. I would like to hear them like that, one after another."

"They are rehearsing, not playing. They have to go over areas of difficulty over and over again. It is part of the process of rehearsing," Boyden reminded Pembroke, trying to hide his irritation.

"Yes, I know, but I can't help it. I want to hear it straight through for once. I have a longing to hear the music in its full glory."

"We'll do it," James agreed. "It will be fun." James conferred with John before directing the musicians. When they finished the short performance, James looked out over the empty concert hall for approval from Pembroke.

"Excellent!" Pembroke clapped his hands together until his palms hurt. As the musicians continued with their rehearsal, Pembroke sat back in his seat. When the musicians once again became engrossed in their work, Pembroke quietly left the concert hall.

The Queen and Caldwell waited for him outside Altmont. Kate reached for his hands as he approached them. She squeezed his hands lightly before slipping one of her hands through the crook of his arm. As she walked in silence between Lord Pembroke and Lord Caldwell, she lowered her head and laid it against Pembroke's shoulder with affection. They walked quietly until the lights of the main castle welcomed them. Kate lifted her head and looked into Pembroke's eyes. "They are good, aren't they?"

"Yes, very." Pembroke confronted Caldwell's scowling face.

"Sir Henry agrees with us. He thinks they are very good," the Queen assured Pembroke. "He still feels the people are not ready for such a different musical flavor. He feels we won't see any return on our investment in them, if they play it all their own way. He may be right." The Queen paused in her stride. "We'll do it anyways." She turned to meet Caldwell's surprise with her warm smile. "We will do it anyways."

The musical group was ready for its first tour before the year ended. The first performance was held in the royal concert hall for the aristocracy. It was a phenomenal success, followed by accomplishment after accomplishment. As the group made its way across Fiara, James carried the crystal wing with him, hidden within his old knapsack. He never told the others about the crystal wing. He secretly placed it into his pocket like a good luck piece before every performance. James was amazed at the speed of their success. As they traveled across the world on their second tour, he felt the momentum of their fame gathering into a greater force. He sensed a heightened magnetism between himself and his audience. The people seemed to love their music. Audience attendance reached maximum capacity in every city in which they played.

By the end of their second tour, popular demand for their music reached an astronomical peak. People crowded the streets and thoroughfares of the cities in which they played. Groups of ardent admirers followed them from city to city. When they returned to Yves, people camped along the castle walls hoping for a glimpse of them. Fiara had never experienced anything like it.

Caldwell was aghast at the clamor. "I don't understand it. Their music is good, but this goes beyond anything I've ever seen. They are being treated like royalty."

"I suppose, to the people, they are a type of royalty," the Queen mused. "I must admit they are refreshing, especially compared to us."

"It is dangerous," Caldwell warned her.

"Perhaps it is dangerous, or perhaps it's not. Their popularity can only help us in the end."

Caldwell fumed over their skyrocketing fame, until the Queen allowed him to initiate a fee charging each individual for admittance to their performances. Caldwell expected the fee to quell their popularity once and for all. Instead, the people seemed even more eager to see the group and hear its music. As Caldwell saw profit flow into the treasury from James's performances, his antagonism toward James waned.

Over the next few years, their fame refused to dampen. Lord Pembroke felt moved to petition the Queen to open negotiations between the monarchy and the two young musicians. As their representative, Lord Pembroke requested monetary rewards never before received by court musicians. Although Caldwell felt certain the Queen would never seriously consider the ludicrous proposal set forth by Pembroke on behalf of James and John, he was wrong. The Queen entered the court into an intense debate concerning the rights of the two musicians who had turned the course of Fiara around with their music. For the first time in his life, Lord Pembroke proved adept in tackling a project. With managerial finesse, he procured a share of the profit from the music they had created and performed. With his heated debates and arduous efforts, he permanently secured James and John's finances.

Over the next year, Pembroke worked diligently to further the political status of the two musicians within the court. In the end, they were each issued a large estate with options to use several tracts of land inherited by the monarchy. With popularity, wealth and access to land a part of their holdings, only the royal titles to their land separated them from the nobility.

When James brought this to John's attention, he shrugged it off. "I don't want to be anything like them. Still, I will take their money and use their land—all they want to send my way."

"What good is any of this if we haven't got the titles?" James insisted. "Without the titles, they can take it all away from us whenever they want, whenever anyone becomes the least bit dissatisfied with us." James snapped his fingers, "Just like that, it's gone."

P.J. Chiuchiolo

"We can't own the titles, James. You know that. You should be satisfied with the wealth. Only the nobility can own titles to land."

"No, once, John. Once, only the nobility owned titles to land."

John raised a dubious eye to his friend. "I'd like to see that, myself." He raised his drinking glass to James and squirmed with apprehension. "That is impossible, isn't it?"

James, touching the crystal wing hidden in his pocket, did not answer him.

12

James smoothed his hair into place, winked at himself in the mirror and feigning a whisper said, "Sir James. It sounds natural enough." He called over his shoulder, "Look at this, John. Do I look noble enough?"

"If vanity determines it, you're plenty noble."

James laughed. He moved across the room and shook John's knee. "Come on and get dressed now or we'll be late. And stop drinking that stuff. It clogs the brain."

"It clears it." John poured a small portion of Grogg into his cup. "I need it to free the enslaved channels of my mind, for my lucid and ingenious prose." He tasted a sip of the Grogg. "So, tell me how this marvelous transformation occurs from musician to nobleman. Do we change as they are handing us the documents or shortly after? If we lose the documents do we immediately revert back to ordinary people or does it take a while? I don't think we should accept those papers until we know for sure, James. After all, didn't they tell us at one of those meetings we had that you had to be born to nobility? They said we couldn't buy it, but they changed their minds. If they changed their minds once, they could again."

"Get dressed, John."

John smirked, "You are losing your sense of humor. No, I'm not feeling noble, James. On occasion, I feel a little noble, but not as a general rule. You are going to have to go this one alone."

"And what will you do?"

"I will vigorously woo a beautiful young lady. In fact, even as the documents are handed to you, I shall culminate the act. You may think of me then, James."

James stared at him, his cold expression attacking John viciously. John seemed unmoved. He added, "Just drop my copy of the documents off at my suite when you are done with the ceremony."

James felt uneasy with John's words to him. Although James expected John to refuse to attend the initiation ceremony, there was a subtle insinuation underlying the words that unnerved him. James shook off his feelings defensively. He had done nothing wrong. As James walked to the reception, he fretted about his friend. It was the Grogg, of course. He had been drinking too much of it again. It slanted his perspective. James turned his thoughts to the ceremony, preparing an excuse for John's absence from the event.

The ceremony completely changed their status at court. They were moved from Altmont into the main castle. New positions as advisors to the artistic orders were created for them, promising advancement one day into the Queen's Counsel. James built a country estate on the shores of Lake Knapp on the land the Queen deeded to him in Eastham. There he spent his leisure time with a young lady from the court, Mary.

Mary's father was a physician from Sumatra. He had been asked to attend the court as a court physician for a five year period, a reward for his superior achievement in the healing arts. It provided him an opportunity to study, use the court facilities and make valuable contacts with court members. Mary had seen James when he first entered the Royal Order of Musicians. She very much wished to know him, but her father was against their association. He avoided introducing James to his daughter. His court appointment held enormous opportunity for Mary and his ambition hoped for a better match for his daughter than a mere court musician.

Through her circle of friends at court, Mary discovered that James had spent some time in Sumatra as a guest of Ena Ishtosh. Knowing Ena, Mary wrote to her asking for her help. Ena was happy to introduce James to Mary. She wrote to James requesting he befriend the young woman. Ena enclosed a letter of introduction for James to use with Mary's father. With a formal letter of introduction from Ena, Mary's father conceded with reluctance. When James gained a higher position in the court with the success of his music, Mary's father began to encourage the match. By the time James received his title, their friendship had become a torrid love affair.

Once James accepted his title, Mary's father sought his honorable intentions for Mary. When James promised a legal commitment to Mary, Mary's father turned his head on their affair, letting it take its natural course. In an attempt to protect

Mary's reputation, they confined the physical aspects of their relationship to the seclusion of his country estate in Eastham. On some occasions, they found it impossible to exercise restraint. In those evenings, they would stealthily risk a meeting in the castle to fulfill their carnal pleasures.

One such evening, as they lie entwined, exhausted from the ravenous interlocking of their lovemaking, a light tapping on the suite door summoned James from his bed. Pembroke waited for him outside the suite, a little anxious and embarrassed for intruding.

Pembroke poked James apologetically and with a cheerful tone said, "Come on, James. It is time again."

"Go on. I am too tired," James grumbled.

"Hurry and dress. I'll wait for you in the lower corridor."

James cussed under his breath, but closed the suite door and dressed trying not to disturb Mary. Pembroke waited for him in the hallway on the first floor. When James arrived, Pembroke led him through the dim halls of the castle and into the dark of its lower chambers.

"This isn't the way we went last time," James whispered, overcome by the stillness of the bleak, deserted chambers.

"No, but it is much safer than the other route." Pembroke led him to a hidden stairwell, disintegrating from lack of upkeep. "Don't worry. It will hold up for us. Move slowly. Imagine, this is the same stairway Pilchard used on his secret rendezvous' with the Queen. I hope your fate turns out better than his did."

"If it doesn't, I have you to thank, Willie. Remember, you helped make all this possible."

Pembroke broke into a benevolent laugh, "Ah, James, I merely suggested a way for you to attain your goals and fulfill that impossible ambition of yours. Quite frankly, I was surprised that she even considered it."

When they reached the top landing, Pembroke shifted his lantern before knocking on the door. As he did, he noticed a troubled look etch across James's face. It touched Pembroke deeply. Pembroke dared hesitate only a moment. He unlocked the door and beckoned James into the room. The next day, James and Mary left without warning for Eastham.

It was several weeks before James broke his seclusion and returned to court. When he did, he immediately went to Pembroke's suite.

"The deal is off, Willie. I relinquish my title."

"Oh, dear, you can't do that, James. You simply can not do that." Pembroke rubbed his chin, his face creasing with worry.

"I can do it. The deal is off. I won't do it anymore."

"You have told Mary."

"No, I haven't told anyone. I just want out of the deal."

Pembroke, his temples drawing taught, begged him, "James, you don't understand. You can't back out now. It is too late."

"She doesn't own me. She only gave me a title and some land. The title is a piece of paper, Willie. It doesn't say that she owns me."

"But you agreed to the conditions, James. You can not go back on your word."

"I haven't gone back on my word. I have given her enough seed to fertilize ten women. I can't help it if it hasn't taken. For all I know, she is barren. She is old. She may be past her years for bearing children. With this agreement, I could remain her personal whore for the rest of her natural life."

"Don't think of it in that way. You are lucky she agreed to this arrangement. She never agreed before this. We need an heir. You are performing a service to your world."

"Look, Willie, you know I am loyal to her, but service to our world was the last thing on my mind when I agreed to it. But, I am really not like that. I don't know what came over me. I am really not like that, deep in my soul." James desperately searched for the words to sway Pembroke to support his decision. "I went into this for the wrong reasons and that is why I have to get out of it."

"You do not seem to understand. It is impossible for you to get out of this agreement. If you go back on your word to her, she can have you imprisoned and even executed."

"On what charge? How would she explain it to the people, Willie? They love us. I would be out before she could bring me to trial."

"Maybe you are right, but I would rather you didn't take the gamble. It would be very embarrassing for the Queen and vitally dangerous to your well being. You are sure to lose, no matter the final outcome. James, I am very fond of you, and so is the Queen. Neither one of us wants any harm to come to you, but you have forgotten one important detail. Your rise to fame has brought you more freedom than most are allowed in Fiara. The final truth is that the Queen does own you, one way or another."

James fell silent with his words. His own silence crushed the air around him, draining him of color and breath. His quiet shock accused Pembroke, moving him to the point of tears. Pembroke tried to maintain composure. He folded his arms, tightly damming the sympathetic emotions from spilling over his eyes. He waited, until James conceded in hushed defeat.

"Good!" Willie's relieved excitement exploded as he grabbed James and hugged him. He patted him on the back and tried to comfort him. "You look tired, James. You are tired, that is all."

"No, I need a change," James' eyes squinted with the pain of defeat. His words were marked by heaviness.

"Then, perhaps you should go to Eastereven. They have invited you to their ball. It is a gala event, and Eastereven lies near the Arca V'ing Enta. It is a magical place that warms the soul. They say anything can happen there. It is beautiful, simply beautiful there. Have you ever been to the Arca V'ing Enta?"

"No, I have always wanted to go. I never could find time."

"Oh, then please go to Eastereven. Everyone should go to Eastereven once in their lifetime."

Venoma

13

For the third night in a week, she awoke crying out, shuddering. It had been happening for some time. She lay under the covers frozen in the darkness, her stomach tight, unable to recall the furtive and elusive dream that created her turmoil. The dream seemed to haunt her again and again. She threw back the covers and made her way in the semidarkness from the bedroom to the outside hallway, inching her way along the corridor, fighting the gloom. An upsurge of fear overcame her. She reversed her course and returned to her suite of rooms. As she entered, she was enveloped in pale light. It calmed her.

She crossed the room and opened the balcony doors. The fresh air drew her onto the balcony. Resting against the railing, her vision wandered across the lawns until she could see a shimmering glimpse of the lake lying beyond the grassy slope and decorative flora of the university yards. The evening lights flickered and danced across the water. She looked toward the mountain at the far side of the lake. She watched the light at its peak spraying the countryside. The soft lights filled her with warmth, chasing away the stark, musty ache from the shadowed corners of her mind. She began to feel safe. On nights like this one, Erin was grateful she lived beneath the Jewel of Light.

Erin lived in the city called Esaunum. Esaunum sprawled across the countryside along the lake bordering the mountain of the Jewel of Light. From anywhere within the boundaries of Esaunum, the light of the Jewel could be seen and felt. It cast a luminous glow across the stone surfaces and grassy parkways of the city, a gentle reminder of the original purpose of the people of Esaunum. The city was born to protect the Jewel and its light. Its original purpose had eroded and was transformed by the passage of time into more practical ideas. Esaunum was a city bustling with ideas; new ideas, brilliant ideas, material ideas. The overflow of ideas was slowly corrupting its people so that even the Jewel of Light had become only another scenic attraction in a world lush with an abundance of natural beauty.

Erin was born in Esaunum. Her grandfather, a lifelong delegate to the World Counsel, had built his home along the lake shore. When he retired from his service, he left the home for his son to use, building a cottage in the countryside beyond the lake in the agricultural community of Durham. It was in the rambling home along the lake that Erin first remembered watching the light of the Jewel. She never wearied of its brilliant hues. It never became commonplace to her as it had become to so many others. She loved the sight of the light gleaming from its mountain sanctuary. It filled her heart with hope, until her spirit longed for fulfillment. Whenever Erin felt troubled, she would look across the lake to the mountain. She would watch throughout the night, until the light entered its morning pattern. In the early morning, the intensity of the light surged, burst, showering the lake with colorful sparkles. The pattern repeated, growing in strength and pulse until the dawn cooled its fiery tempo and morning soothed the pervasive character of its light.

Erin watched from the balcony of her university suite as the light decorated the sky. The night vigil calmed her. In the morning, she struggled through her classes. She spent the afternoon along the lake. When the sun hung low over the water, she returned to the dormitory to change for the evening meal. After dressing, she walked the length of the campus green and met her sister at the northern dining room.

They chose a secluded table. Without hesitating, Erin confided that her restless nights had returned. "I don't know why I let these dreams bother me. I don't usually remember anything specific about them, but this time," Erin grabbed a piece of paper from her sister's leaflet, "I remember this." She drew two rings overlapping each other. "I think it means two worlds, two worlds converging upon each other like two rings, like this." She turned the paper toward her sister, pointing to the symbol. "That's all I can remember, except that there seems to be something else in the dream—an energy or maybe a source—something very powerful lying somewhere beyond the darkness of the dream. It hangs there and makes me feel like I've forgotten something or someone. It's very important. I don't know why. It's the strangest feeling."

Janus scowled. "It's just two rings."

"Yes, I know, but it leaves me with such an uneasy feeling. I feel as if something has been left undone."

"Anything could make you feel like that." Janus let her words knife the air.

"You think I am being foolish."

Janus smoothed the drawing, trying unsuccessfully to cover her harsh, doubtful tone. "No, I don't think you are foolish. I don't know what this symbol means. You could have seen it anywhere. I must have seen it in a dozen places."

"Where have you seen it?"

"I don't know. I can't remember right this moment, but I know I must have seen it in a lot of places. It is not an unusual symbol."

Erin took the drawing from Janus and traced its lines in exasperation. Finally, she conceded, "You are right. It's a common symbol. I'm being stupid." She laughed at herself. "It's only a dream anyways."

Erin let it go. She allowed silence to separate them. Within the comfort of the silence, she felt the persistent feeling diminish; but before they got up to return to the dormitory, it reared again, nagging her beneath her consciousness, an uneasy feeling of expectation ever so slightly pinging against her soul.

It was days before she settled again into a normal routine, forgetting her lonely vigil in the night. Her wasted time had left her behind in her studies. She began to frequent the library trying to catch up with her assignments. One evening near the end of the academic term, her studies were interrupted by the excited voice of Janus.

"Erin, come here; come over here. I have something to show you." Janus stood within a group of students near the back of the library, waving to Erin with violent excitement. As Erin drew close to her, Janus grabbed her arm and guided her through the crowded aisles of the library into a back room. She pulled Erin up a narrow spiral staircase, furiously spewing words at her. "You are not going to believe what I found. I was late with my paper and he decided to put me to work. You could say we agreed that if I helped clean up some of his old papers back here, he would accept the paper as if it were handed in on time. Well, you are not going to believe what I found in one of those old boxes. I couldn't believe it at first. Look." Janus handed Erin a parchment that smelled musty from storage. "Here it is, right here. It's the symbol from your dream—an ancient symbol from Venoma's past. You see, it says it right here."

Erin looked at the parchment. Relief filled her as she saw the two interwoven rings and read the words, "an ancient symbol from Venoma's past." What the symbol meant, Erin didn't know. The parchment, a one page exhibit of symbols, never explained its meaning. The librarians didn't seem to know either, and a search for other references in the library proved futile.

"At least you know it's a real symbol," Janus consoled her. It was not enough for Erin. She needed to know more, and she discerned who might know the answers to the questions plaguing her mind.

Arian Dartaun was a quiet man of small stature. His strong presence of character more than compensated for his diminutive size. He had devoted most of his life in service on the World Counsel, the primary governing body of Venoma. Even in Counsel, he spoke infrequently. When he did speak, his words were always taken seriously. He was known to have an amazing intuition. Most people considered it a gift. He was not surprised when his granddaughter arrived in the middle of a school week and broached the subject of dreams with hidden meanings. He was surprised when she drew the two overlapping rings and asked if he knew their meaning.

"Why are you interested in this symbol?" he asked, hiding a forbidding concern.

"I dreamt it, and it has hung over me so intensely that I couldn't forget about it. I thought maybe you would know more about it. Janus found an old parchment in a back room of the library that says it has to do with the past. It didn't say anything more than that."

"It does have to do with our past," Arian spoke slowly, hesitating to reveal more, "a very ancient past—a past most have forgotten." He seemed to study the simple lines as his mind slipped into deep thought. His granddaughter followed each movement of his eyes and facial muscles unguarded, until he spoke again. "Let me think about it for a few days," he finally said.

The very next day, he called Erin into his study. He folded the sketch and wrote a short note on the back of the paper. Returning the paper to Erin, he cautioned her. "It's not usually allowed, but I will bend the rules this one time. I'll get you into the archives. When you get there, give this note to Jason."

14

The building housing the archives was hidden in the forest more than a day's journey from Esaunum. Most people in Venoma didn't know it existed. The building sight had been carefully chosen for its removed location. The design blended into the forest surroundings. Its color camouflaged it further, discouraging accidental discovery. Admission to the building could only be obtained through the World Counsel. Admission was rarely granted.

The ancient texts stored within the archives reviewed the history of Venoma from many perspectives. Many of the volumes contradicted each other, muddying any attempt to portray an accurate historical account of the world. The volumes containing the legends of the Jewel were even more confusing. Each volume illustrated a variation on its background and each gave it a mythical appearance. Somewhere along the way, the real purpose of the Jewel had been clouded and the reason for the building of the Great Wall surrounding its mountainous seat distorted. No one knew for sure how the Jewel had come to sit upon the mountain top, nor why its light shone endlessly without fuel to spark it. A strict tradition of guarding the Jewel as a material treasure gradually developed, as knowledge of its true meaning and power withered. From its very ancient beginnings, the World Counsel had always been in agreement. It was better the people forget. With the help of each successive Counsel, time erased the impact the Jewel once had upon Venoma.

Erin traveled by horseback to a small hamlet several hours from the archive sight. There, she roomed with relatives of a friend. In the morning, she journeyed through the forest trail, following the detailed instructions from her grandfather. Along the trail, Erin was confronted by several guards. When she showed them her pass, a guard brought her to the entrance to the archive, unlocked the gate and led her through a small receiving room to a stone stairwell. At the second floor, he took her down a long narrow hallway to another door. He knocked on the door with loud, sure beats and left her before it opened.

A thin man opened the door, irritated, a frown covering his face. He peered down the hallway and scrutinized Erin without speaking. Ignoring her, he yelled down the hallway, "Is this a joke? I don't think it's funny." He listened with impatience for an answer. When none came, he addressed Erin, "You better get back down there. You can get into trouble for coming in here like this. Tell them I don't think it is funny letting you in here. All of you could be in a lot of trouble."

"I have a pass. I'm supposed to give this to Jason," Erin showed him the pass and folded drawing.

"Let me see those." The man grabbed the pass and drawing from her. A smile crossed his face when he looked at the pass. "I haven't seen one of these since I first came here. It looks authentic. Welcome," he reached for Erin's hand shaking it in excitement. "Wait. Let me see what this says." He released her hand to read the note on the drawing.

"I'm supposed to give that to Jason."

"Don't worry. I'm Jason." The man toyed with the wire-rim glasses sitting along the bridge of his nose. "I know your grandfather. He says I'm to help you make sense of this symbol. It's an unusual request; but for him I'll do it. Come along, then. You can only stay a few hours by law and it will take more than that to read the volume you need." He let her inside, locking the door behind her.

Erin followed Jason into an expansive room jammed with aisles of shelves stacked with papers, boxes and books. He moved up and down the aisles without reason, stopping occasionally to pull a volume from a shelf. Clicking his tongue, he took her by her arm and seated her at a small table squirreled along a clutter of shelves in the back of the room. "Here. You wait here. I must have misplaced it. It has to be here somewhere. I probably filed it in the wrong place." He hurried out of sight. The sporadic sound of his scuffling feet and falling books broke the otherwise stale silence of the room. Without warning, his head popped through the shelves next to her. "Here it is." He pushed aside a box sliding a heavy volume through the shelf to her. "That's the one you want to look at. If you need me, give me a call." He disappeared behind the boxes and books again.

Erin ran a hand over the rough, dulled cover of the volume. Her fingers played with its raised impression of the interwoven rings. Her heart raced a little as she opened the cover to its dry, yellowed pages and began to read. The prose fascinated her with its foreign rhythms and staid verse.

Long ago, the legend told, the Arca V'ing Enta rose from the foundation of the sea to span the air, and the Jewel of Light with its crystal wings was placed on the mountain for all to see. Venoma was not cut off from other worlds then, nor from the beings of light that lay beyond the Arca V'ing Enta. The Lady of the Sun was a being of light. She frequently visited Venoma and guided the people toward their goal of spiritual peace. She was the caretaker of the Jewel. The people depended on her wisdom. Those people in Venoma with higher understanding were taught by the lady to use the power of the crystal wings to move freely through the Arca V'ing Enta. With each venture through its mystical body, they gained greater insight and inner wisdom. They carried this wisdom into their daily lives and shared it with those unable to travel through the Arc's beatific curtain. Spiritual truth reigned in Venoma, in a culture rich with joy and founded in peace, manifested by an abundance of gifts among the people.

All was well until a leader emerged from within the generations who secretly longed to possess the crystal wings. He went to the base of the Jewel and tried to force the wings from their setting. The act was cataclysmic. The sea shuddered with a permanent disturbance making it impossible to ever pass through its waters again. The land shook and upturned with a roar echoing even through the channels of the Arca V'ing Enta. The Arca V'ing Enta closed. The Jewel formed a protective force around the remaining wing. The world filled with a dark and destructive force. The leader disappeared and with him went one half of the crystal wings. With the wings broken, Venoma plunged into an age of guttural confusion and fear. In their fear, the people built a great wall around the mountain to prevent access to the Jewel of Light and its remaining crystal wing.

Erin read the legend, engrossed, until the sound of Jason rustling papers nearby disturbed her concentration. "Do you know anything about this?" she asked him.

"My you're a fast reader. Yes, I do." Jason leaned close to her, finding her place in the volume. His hands caressed the pages. He tapped the page with an index finger. "Yes, yes, it's Justlevenoma, *The Legends of Justlevenoma.* The volume is marked by the interwoven rings."

"You've read it."

"I've read it many, many times. There is something about it that captures me," Jason sighed.

"You think this is true?" Erin looked up at him searching.

"As close to true as we shall ever get. You must remember that legends are handed down by word of mouth for who knows how long before they are actually recorded. We have no way to validate its accuracy or authenticity. Of course, we see the light shining from the Jewel and have laws establishing severe penalty for attempting to pass over the Great Wall. Death, no questions asked. No need for a trial. There isn't a soul in Venoma who doesn't know at least that about the wall. We have guarded the wall for our entire history. It's a part of our beliefs, our culture and our law. The rest is better to forget. As best we can."

"I never realized there were crystal wings at the base of the Jewel," Erin looked down at the pages in front of her.

"No one else does either. This is the only legend that mentions them. And if this one is true, there is only one wing left. You see," he lowered his voice. Tightening his facial muscles, he looked around the cluttered room. "The Counsel has always agreed that it is better the people forget about the real history of the Jewel. I was surprised you were allowed to see this volume. If I hadn't seen Arian's own handwriting myself, I wouldn't have let you in. It can only lead to trouble, if you ask me." His eyes narrowed. He walked back to his stack of papers.

Erin watched him busy himself with his work before returning to the volume. Once again, she was absorbed in its compelling story. She had not yet finished its bulky contents when Jason began turning down the lights in the room.

"I'm very sorry," he said as he dimmed the light next to her table, "but I'm going to have to ask you to leave now. It's truly been a pleasure. I'm not allowed visitors here very often."

Erin closed the volume gathering it into her arms. "I'll put this away for you. Where does it go?"

"Don't bother. I'll do it later," Jason took the book from her and laid it on the table. "I'll have plenty of time later to do it."

"I thought you were leaving."

"No." He placed a hand along her shoulder as he moved her through the narrow aisles to the door. "I have a small apartment in the back. I'm not allowed to leave." After unlocking the door, he took her hand and shook it. "It's been a pleasure," he said, a note of sadness escaping in the tone of his voice as he closed the door. "I hope you have a safe journey back to Esaunum."

The legends of Justlevenoma quelled the compelling nature of Erin's dreams. When she returned to school, restfulness overtook her. As the last days of her studies for the year approached, she made plans to spend the interim break at her parent's home along the lake shore. Her first days home were spent swimming, boating and sunning herself. By the second week, the archives seemed a distant past and Justlevenoma a pleasant tale to tuck away with the rest of her studies.

15

The soulful call of a water bird penetrated the deep comfort of Erin's sleep. Within its voice, she heard her name whispered, like a soft harmony tingling along the inner tones of the bird, gently echoing into her mind. She felt a light vibration along the bedcovers teasing her awake. Erin pushed back the covers and peered into the soft light illuminating her room. As her eyes fathomed its growing intensity, the light concentrated at the foot of her bed; and from within the center of its brilliance, Erin saw the form of a woman appear. Erin backed herself over her pillows, wedging herself against the headboard and wall.

"Erin, come down off the pillows," the woman said in a soothing voice, her smile glowed with understanding.

"No," Erin squeezed through her tightened throat.

The woman, still smiling, moved closer allowing her light to fall across Erin. As her light brushed along her skin, Erin felt her body rushing with warmth and a feeling of lightheartedness washed her. "The Lady of the Sun," she thought.

"Yes," the woman answered her before the question could pass Erin's lips. "And I've come a long way to speak with you."

Erin moved to the edge of the bed. Her legs dangled over the covers. The silky smoothness of her nightclothes rubbed the skin along her calves. She looked down at her legs, highlighted by the light from the woman, and lightly pinched the skin on her left thigh. She looked back up at the lady of light. "I don't understand. I must be dreaming."

The lady looked deeply into her eyes. "Sleep is an unusual state of consciousness, Erin. It seems we are shut off from all that is outside of us, periods of deep rest and periods of dreams. Sometimes, dreams are only the mind sharpening and exercising its capabilities. Self created illusions. And other times ... At other times, dreams can hold the windows to a higher consciousness. When you open your heart, you open your windows." The lady reached out with open hands to her. "I have heard you've been searching for the truth about the past. I understand you have read the Legends of Justlevenoma." The lady mused. "The legends are all clouded with false ideas, but Justlevenoma..."

"It's true, then," Erin whispered with conviction.

"When the crystal wings at the base of the Jewel were broken, the people allowed fear to overtake them. They called to me asking what they should do. They never heard the answer. Instead, they built a great wall around the mountain of the Jewel." The lady closed her eyes, touching the fingertips of her hands together. "Go to the mountain, Erin. Take the crystal wing from the base of the Jewel. Tell no one. Keep it close to you. When the time is right, you will know what to do."

"I can't go to the mountain. No one is allowed on the mountain. They'll kill me."

"Go to the Jewel, Erin."

"It's impossible. No one has ever made it to the Jewel. Everyone who has tried failed. They were killed and their tortured bodies placed on public display. Everyone is required to view them by law. I know. I remember seeing someone as a child. Only once, but I have never forgotten it. I shall never forget it." Erin's voice caught with emotion. Tears sprung against her lashes.

"Sometimes, Erin, we have to risk everything. Trust your heart. Your heart knows the truth. Go to the mountain. You will see the good it will bring."

"I'll never get past the force shield and the great wall..." her words of protest drifted as her body filled with the heaviness of sleep.

The Lady of the Sun smiled, "Oh, Erin. Walls are built by men of little faith."

When Erin awoke, the bedcovers lay strewn away from her body. Morning dampness chilled her to the bone. She pulled herself onto her elbows. The fresh smell of lake water filled the air around her. She breathed. The call of a water bird echoed across her senses. She remembered the night and the lady of light.

"I must have been dreaming," she thought out loud, dispelling the pangs that butted against her inner self.

She turned onto her side, pulling the covers over her head. The words of the lady resounded through her mind. The image of light burned her memory as she got out of bed and went to the window. The early morning sun swallowed the darkness from the edge of the lake. She leaned out the window trying to catch the view of the mountain holding the Jewel, but she only glimpsed a few sparkles from the last of the night sky.

Doubt filled Erin's mind. Her visit to the Archives and the volume she read about the ancient legends could easily have provoked a dream about the legendary being called the Lady of the Sun. Her stomach churned at the thought. Her vision seemed so real. She struggled within the swirling milieu of her skepticism and fear until the stirring of a deep faith within her heart overcame her. In the end, she could not help herself. She listened to her heart and went to the mountain.

When she drew near to the mountain base, a compelling instinct overtook her guiding her away from the accessible paths. She followed a small overgrown footpath winding through a stretch of dense woodland. The path seemed to weave away from the mountain. Despite its confusing direction, Erin remained on course. By the time she reached the first rise in the land, she was already fatigued. Again an invisible force directed her. She left the path at a right angle to the rise in the land and made her way through the thick brush. The terrain grew steep and treacherous. Erin slipped along the jagged rocks overgrown with moss and green brush, falling against their sharp surfaces, abrading and bruising the skin underneath her clothing. She climbed ever higher until the structure of the wall loomed like a towering giant blocking her upward mobility.

The massive darkness of the stone wall against the light of day overshadowed her small figure, threatening her with its immovable presence. Bearing right, she moved along its parameter. When the space for her footing narrowed, she pressed her body close against the harsh stone surface of the wall. Her footing tightened. She dragged her body across the wall trying to avoid a fall down the steep embankment. The sound of the surf below her beat against her ears in a warning. Erin held her balance, pressing tight against the rock of the wall. As her hand rested on a flaw in its even surface, she pushed against it in her fear. The large rock underneath her hand caved into the inner sanctuary of the wall. Breathing hard with disbelief and excitement, Erin squeezed her body through the small opening. Falling onto the cool grass, she fell asleep.

When Erin awoke, her eyes were filled with the brilliant colors of an exotic bird. Its low pitched melody chirped in her ears as it cocked its head teasing her. As she moved into wakefulness, it abruptly hesitated in its song. Spreading its wings, it fluttered into the air a few feet above the meadow, circling at a distance before swooping and returning to perch next to her. Still watching the bird, Erin rose and made her way through the grassy slope of the meadow toward the mountain top. The Jewel shimmered above her in the stronghold of its rocky setting, its light blinding and brilliant even in the clear light of day. The colorful songbird to which she had awakened rested at its base within the glowing light of the Jewel.

Erin, stilled by the image before her, watched the bird take flight low to the ground, landing in the grass next to her. Hopping, it took flight back to the base of the Jewel. Returning to her in its low flight pattern, it once again broke into song. Erin looked at the bird at her feet and then to the Jewel. A few puzzling moments passed before she realized that the force shield was gone. The way to the Jewel was open and safe for her.

16

Erin returned from the mountain dusty and bruised. She hid the wing in one of her music boxes and placed it in a bureau drawer underneath her clothes. After hiding the wing, she tended to her scrapes and bruises in secret. No one suspected she had been in the sanctuary of the Jewel of Light.

For days, Erin tried to forget the crystal wing buried at the bottom of the drawer. Time and time again, she returned to her room pacing back and forth. After a week passed, she removed the crystal wing from the music box. She took a gold chain from an old necklace, strung it through the crystal wing and placed the chain with the wing around her neck for safekeeping. Drained from the tension of the week, she sank into the cushioned comfort of her bedroom chair. In its billowy softness, she relaxed until she fell asleep. Through restfulness, Erin felt herself pulled into flight. When she opened her eyes, she stood on the outskirts of the Arca V'ing Enta. Erin scanned the unfamiliar landscape. The wooded vista was marred by a dilapidated hut. Erin's ears were hammered by the jarring sound of a man's voice.

"Benjamine, Benjamine. Bring that over here. No. No. Not that one, the other one. Yes. Yes. Bring it over here," the man's voice trailed off into sputtering.

Dazed and unsure, Erin followed the sound to the back of the hut. In the backyard, she was struck by the sight of a massive structure composed of mud, clay, branches and an array of brush. A stocky figure hung precariously onto a homemade, rickety ladder. As the man leaned into his work, he furiously patted and prodded, molding the mud.

"Will you look at this? This is wonderful. Just wonderful," he burst into excited delight. With a fevered pitch, he dove back into his struggle with the mud.

Erin stood quietly to one side watching him poke and smooth the mud before speaking to him. "Excuse me," she finally dared venture. "Could you tell me where I am?"

"Don't interrupt me," the man exploded, his body quivering with exasperation. "Can't you see I'm working?" Without hesitation, he returned to the mud.

Erin watched him digging and molding in the wet medium for a long time. His movements were intense, focused, broken on occasion by a "Yes, yes" or an "Ah". When he finally stepped away from the piece, he studied it from many angles. "Benjamine, come here and see what I've done!" he exclaimed. He turned to Erin. "Come. Come," he motioned her with childish excitement. "Come look at what I've done." He maneuvered Erin gracefully around the monstrous pile. "You see. Well, what do you think?"

Erin carefully considered the heap before her. "It's ...interesting," she gave as a safe opinion. She looked closer noticing an appealing uniqueness in its design. "It's incredibly textured," she added with appreciation.

"Yes," he burst out with glee, "Exactly. It is interesting in every respect." The artist stood breathing in deep gulps. He looked with glazed eyes at his work. Erin stood beside him at a respectful distance, following him as he moved about the yard. He longed to take in every aspect of his labor. He caressed each curve and branch with his eyes. When the shadow of approaching evening teased his work, he called out with fatigue in his voice, "Benjamine. Please make a fire. We have a guest this evening."

As Erin and the artist walked to the hut, a slender boy scooted in between them. His hat was too big, as were his pants and boots. "This is Benjamine," the artist explained to Erin.

Benjamine shook his head hurrying to gather the firewood strewn around the yard. He stumbled into the hut ahead of them, dumping the firewood into the center of the room. By the time Erin and the artist sat down, Benjamine had started a fire and placed a pot of water in its heat. Erin watched the boy hustle about the hut in a futile attempt to straighten the disarray.

"Benjamine is my helper," the artist informed Erin. "Now, what is your name?"

"Erin," she answered with a soft voice, shying from his frank gaze.

"Erin. It sounds straight and to the point. I like it. But you're not from around here. I can tell. I knew it right away, out there. But my work had me captured. It always comes first." The artist's eyes followed the movements of his helper, Benjamine. He crooked his mouth with secretive knowing, "You have to excuse Benjamine's nervous ways. You see, he can't see you so he thinks I'm talking to myself again." The artist tried to hide his mirth.

A shudder of fear passed within Erin. "He can't see me?"

"No, he can't see you. He can't see you or hear you at all."

"You mean he can't see or hear you either."

"No. He can hear and see me quite well. Right, Benjamine? It's you he has a problem with. He can't hear or see you at all."

"How can that be? You can see me, can't you?"

"Of course, I can. I'm talking with you." The artist rested his hands on his lap resisting his frustration with the girl. Rolling his shoulders to relax himself, he leaned closer to her in an amiable pose. "Erin, I hear and see you just fine. You understand, as an artist, my senses are finely tuned. Benjamine and the others, well…" he slapped his hands against his thighs, "And where are you from?" Examining her carefully, he concluded, "From beyond the Arca V'ing Enta, no doubt. Your hair, your clothing, and the ornament you wear. No, you don't have to tell me. I can sense it's true. You've come to see Fiara.

This is so exciting for me." The artist clapped his hands together.

"Where is this Fiara?" Erin stuttered, confused.

"Why, right here, right here. This is Fiara. This is Eastereven, Erin. The most beautiful part of Fiara is right here. You've come to the most beautiful part of our world."

"But where is your world?"

"Right here, along the Arca V'ing Enta. That magnificent bow of colored energy! You are at Eastereven, Erin. Eastereven is infamous for its breathtaking views of the Arca V'ing Enta, lauded for its gala dances and social affairs. And that's where we'll start showing you our world. Yes, it only makes sense. It's the perfect time. We'll start here at Eastereven. Benjamine, get my things together. I'm going to the ball."

"You never go to the ball, Sir," Benjamine stoutly objected.

"Of course, I never go to the ball. But, tonight I have a guest, and she's come a long ways, I'm sure. She needs to experience as much of Fiara as possible. And what better way than the Eastereven Ball? Get my coat. Get my hat. I'm telling you, Benjamine, tonight I am going to the ball!"

Benjamine jumped to comply with the artist. He dug through a pile of clothes in a corner dragging a large, dusty topcoat from under the sheaves. Dropping the coat onto the floor, he ran to a corner of the hut. Hopping on tiptoes, he grabbed a hat from the shelf, dusting its brim as he handed it to the artist. Benjamine smoothed the artist's hair, and then helped him into his outerwear.

He walked with the artist out of the hut. "No, Benjamine," the artist admonished him. "I need you to watch over my work this evening while I accompany this young lady to the ball. Will you do that for me?"

Benjamine prodded the dirt with his feet. With reluctance, he agreed.

"Thank you, Benjamine. You are a true friend. I trust no one else with my work." The artist shook Benjamine's hand. They exchanged a look of mutual respect and devotion. The artist heaved a sigh, a tear wetting the corner of his eye. Mustering his passion, he flourished a hand into the air. "We're gone," he bellowed and charged through the forest with Erin close behind him.

The large, stone hall hosting the Eastereven ball loomed out of the dense forest like a primitive fortress. Its grand ballrooms, spanning several floors, melded into courtyards and balconies overlooking the waterfalls and Finger Lakes of Eastereven. The water of the lakes and waterfalls seemed to intersect and empty into the Arca V'ing Enta from an array of swirling pools. The spray from the waterfalls played with the light from the Arc, creating colorful dancing lights. The fine spray from the waterfalls diffused the color into blending patterns with deep textures.

On the evening of the Eastereven ball, the air was always filled with excitement and the area overflowed with guests. The free ball attracted people from all walks of life and all parts of Fiara. Young, old, rich, and poor crowded the ballrooms, many dressed in their finest garments, or the best they could manage to buy or borrow. When Erin noticed the lavish dress of many of the guests, she resisted the artist's efforts to motion her forward through the crowd.

"I'm not dressed for this," she protested his prodding.

"Of course not," the artist said with patient vexation. "Your clothes are all wrong and your hair. It's beautiful, but not at all in style. No one can see you, so what does it matter?" He waved her toward a small ballroom adjacent to the main balcony. They made their way to the front of the dance floor. Standing to one side, they watched the dancers move gracefully across the floor. The artist pointed to the musicians. "Those are the Royal Players. They've come all the way across Fiara from the Queen's castle to play for this event. She sends some of the best court musicians available for our ball." The artist extended his arm to Erin. "Shall we dance?"

Looking beside her, Erin noticed several people gawking at the artist. Trying to ignore them, she curtsied, politely mimicking the other woman dancers around her. Placing a hand along his arm, she accompanied the artist onto the dance floor. He led her steps in a dramatic style, emphasizing his joy with verbal glee. As they danced, some people looked at the artist with amusement. Others watched his wild antics with fear or disgust.

"Isn't this fun!" he called out boisterously to everyone he passed. Some of the dancers laughed. Many agreed.

Sir James McCautry agreed with him. The sight of the old man twirling around the ballroom floor by himself made him laugh. It was the first honest and open laugh he'd enjoyed in a long time. Every time the artist passed him, James acknowledged him, encouraging him to continue his gleeful act. Consumed with delight, James and Mary removed themselves to the side of the dance floor to watch the artist dance. As James watched the artist weave in-between the crowd of dancers, he saw a young woman appear. Her graceful figure danced along with the artist, keeping time with his steps and buoyant choreography. James was taken by the sight of her. He felt mysteriously drawn to her, as if he knew her. "Who is she?" he asked in a whispered, troubled voice.

"Who is who?" Mary returned as she clapped her hands in rhythm to the dance, trying to catch sight of the artist.

"The one dancing with that old man," James pointed toward the artist.

"James, no one is dancing with the old man. That's what makes it so funny." Mary reached out to catch the artist's hand as he twirled by her.

James caught Erin's eyes with his own as she moved past him. His heart quickened, as he felt his emptiness filling with her being. Erin stopped dancing. She looked at him from between the swirling figures of the dancers, unable to take her eyes from him. The artist blocked her view. "Come on. It's time we leave." He herded her toward the crowd on the opposite side of the ballroom.

"He saw me." Erin, stunned, moved where the artist directed her.

"Yes. I don't know how, but I'm afraid he did. We better get you out of here. This can only cause us trouble." He escorted her through the crowded hallway. When they reached the outdoors, they broke into a run.

James pushed his way through the crowd on the dance floor, trying to keep the artist and the girl in his sight. He chased them through the woodland path until it opened into a clearing near the artist's hut. He caught up with them only in time to see Erin's light figure disappear into the Arca V'ing Enta.

Erin awoke drenched with perspiration. Her heart beat rapidly. It was difficult to catch her breath. Her body felt weighted. When she was able to move, she took the crystal wing from around her neck and returned it to the music box. She placed it into the top drawer of the bureau. "I'll take it back," she thought as she closed the drawer. "I'll take it back tomorrow."

17

Rose Windham strapped the golden body of her wind instrument across the blade of her left shoulder and defiantly gathered the music sheets from the music stand in front of her. She was not a puppet for Henry Caldwell. Her lithe body vibrated the message as she crossed the room.

"We're not done with practice," the instructor challenged her.

"I'm done," Rose scoffed without bothering to turn her head to address him.

She left the building, heading across the courtyard to James's practice suite. The sound of music drifting from the open windows of the suite told her James had returned from Eastereven. When she reached the practice suite, she quietly opened the door. She eased herself into a chair, trying not to disrupt his concentration and removed a flask from her pocket.

As she listened to him play, she sipped the contents of the flask, moving to the rhythms filling the room.

"What are you doing out of class so soon?" James leaned on the piano scribbling an adjustment to the music he was writing.

"He let us out early."

"Don't lie to me, Rose."

"I'm not lying," Rose opened her hands, pleading he accept.

"You're lying," he said with assurance, still concentrating on his work.

Rose leaned back in her chair. With a sardonic smile, she shrugged her shoulders and took another swig from her flask. Her attention wandered.

"Will you listen to this?" James interrupted her.

"Sure." Rose straightened. She loved being the first to hear his new work.

Rose Windham had been brought to Court as a child, shortly after her father's death. Her presence at Court was the result of an arrangement her grandfather had made with the Queen. It was obvious to everyone talent was not a factor in her selection for the Music Order. Rose was the first to admit she lacked true creative talent. It didn't matter to Rose. She never had a choice. Rose grew up in the Music Order under Henry Caldwell's critical eye. To survive, Rose honed the one gift she did possess: the ability to overlook criticism directed towards her. She developed a working knowledge of music and played without giving credence to the ample criticism offered her.

Her persistence bore fruit for her. Over the years, she developed an unusual style heaped with grit. Her fellow musicians, growing accustomed to her unavoidable presence at their affairs, often adapted their music to her simple style. The greatest surprise came from the people. As Rose's voice bloomed from a childlike squawk into a booming gravel voice, she developed a large, consistent following.

Rose was still a young girl when James arrived at Court. She remembered the thrill of watching the Queen introduce him and had waited in line to meet him that evening. He had been especially attentive to the little girl who seemed misplaced amongst the crowd of musicians and nobility. She eventually attached herself to him and began to tag along for some of his rehearsals. James was compassionate with her and patient with her often misdirected passion.

As Rose listened to James sing and play his new song, she leaned closer to him. It was a love song, haunting and beautiful. Rose was taken by the piece. She watched James sing, imagining herself as the object of his desire.

"It's beautiful. Maybe the best you've done." Rose longed to hear the song again. She checked her craving.

"You really like it."

"Yes, of course. It makes me wonder who inspired you."

"A dream, I think." James chuckled in bewilderment.

"Not Mary," Rose blurted out. She took another swig from the flask. "It doesn't remind me of Mary."

"What are you drinking?" James diverted her by grabbing the flask. He smelled it, holding off her protests. "What? Rose, this is Grogg. Where did you get this stuff?"

"A friend gave it to me. Give it back," Rose wretched the flask from him.

"You're too young to drink that."

"Everyone at court drinks it."

"Not everyone, Rose."

"Well, everyone except you, then," Rose chided James. She reluctantly went to an open window and held the flask out of it. She looked at James teasing for permission.

"Go ahead. Do the right thing," James encouraged her.

Rose poured the Grogg out the window returning the empty flask to her pocket. "Okay, so now will you play that song for me again? I'd like to learn it." Rose took her instrument to mouth blowing a harsh note towards James.

James laughed. He playfully grabbed for her instrument, and then spun back to his piano. He dove into a rollicking piece challenging Rose to keep up to him. When she struggled with the timing, he eased the tempo giving her an edge and crossed into his new song with an improvised musical bridge. Rose stopped playing her instrument. Tears sprung into her eyes as she listened to the song. Her young heart swam in its soft message of love. The melody stayed with her even as she crossed the courtyard to John's suite. John sat playing guitar, contemplating a verse of poetry he'd written.

"I need more Grogg," Rose informed him without hesitating. She handed him her empty flask.

"What do you mean? I just gave you a whole flask yesterday. You couldn't have used it already."

"James had me dump it."

"It figures. You know better than to show it to James."

"I was drinking it," Rose pouted.

"Well, drink this where he won't see you." John tossed a full flask to her. "You didn't tell him where you got it."

"I told him a friend gave it to me. He didn't press me about whom."

"And he doesn't need to know who, all right?"

Rose slipped the flask into a pocket shaking her head in agreement. She went to the door. After opening it, she paused. "James has a new song. It's really good."

John watched Rose leave the room, wondering why her news made him feel unhappy. He picked up his guitar and began to play.

After Rose left John's suite, she sat in the hall her back against the wall, listening for the first sounds of his discontent. Notes filled the air wafting the evening breeze until a melody mushroomed into concrete form. Rose felt stilled in her amazement of the creative process. She listened envious of the sound, longing for a part in its production. Hunger finally prompted her to break her lonely vigil and make her way to the dining hall.

"Sir Henry's looking for you," Lord Pembroke scolded her as he hurried through the dining room. When she ignored his warning, he dragged a chair to the table and sat next to her. "I saw him a while ago in the castle. He is not happy with you at all. He's received reports from your instructors that you are not following protocol for your station."

"I'm an artist. I don't have to follow protocol." Rose feigned a disgruntled growl as she stuffed her mouth with food.

"You're still considered a novice and you are expected to follow the rules. You're heading for trouble if you think you can buck Sir Henry. You should know that by now."

Rose raised her eyes in sarcasm continuing her meal.

"Well, I've warned you anyway. I'm on my way to see James right now. To hear how he enjoyed Eastereven. It was his first time there."

"He's writing a song," Rose said through a mouthful. "You probably shouldn't bother him."

"He's writing a song! Marvelous! Then the trip did him some good. Good. Good." Lord Pembroke tipped back in his chair.

"John, too," Rose added smugly.

"John is writing, too? That is good news. They've been in a low spot for a while. It's good to hear the creative juices are stirring again." Pembroke sat back, thoughtful, watching Rose finish the last mouthfuls of her meal.

Pembroke liked her youthful rebelliousness. From her short cropped hair and the men's trousers she sported to the spicy clarity of the songs she chose to sing, Rose displayed her own unique and daring style. Caldwell had been lenient with her as she grew—perhaps too lenient. Pembroke was not the only one who realized the danger of her flamboyant individuality. Many at Court guarded against the day her obstinate rebelliousness would change from being socially appealing to intolerable. Caldwell was obligated to temper, if not curb, her before she got out of control. Pembroke knew it would be difficult for Rose now to accept limits that were not self-imposed.

"Aren't you the least bit worried that Caldwell is looking for you?" Lord Pembroke tested.

"Henry wouldn't think of looking for me here. He wouldn't be caught dead in this dining hall, Willie. You know that."

"It seems Chad would." Pembroke drew her attention to a door on the far side of the room.

"I better go." Rose dodged her way to a nearby door before Chad could catch her.

Chad approached Pembroke bristling. "Excuse me, Lord Pembroke. Would you know where Rose has gone? I saw her a moment ago speaking with you."

"Yes, she was here a moment ago. She took off for no apparent reason. She didn't mention where she was going. Could I help you find her?"

"No, No, thank you, Sir. It's good of you to offer, but it's my job to find her and find her I will."

Lord Pembroke, alight with pleasure, doubted it would be an easy job.

ARCA V'ING ENTA

18

"Ah, Benjamine," the artist grunted settling onto the ground. He kicked his feet out from under him, stretching his legs. Benjamine handed him a bowl of food. The artist's sight wandered about the yard resting on his sculpture. "It still looks really good, don't you think? Notice the way the rain has etched its own artistry into the piece. I may have outdone myself with that one." The artist and Benjamine leaned on their elbows admiring the enormous sculpture of mud, sticks and twigs.

"That one stays here," the artist finally sighed in his thoughtful repose. "It's too big to move away."

"I wouldn't sell it, Sir," Benjamine advised.

"You're right. I couldn't sell it. It's genius, pure genius." The artist lifted his bowl of food and began to eat. He chewed slowly, engrossed with the sculpture before him.

A crashing of horse hoofs through the woods alongside the hut startled them. The rider pulled his steed to a halt in front of the sculpture. He walked his horse to one side of it, examining it thoroughly. "Are you the owner?" he asked looking first at the artist and then to Benjamine.

"I'm the owner," the artist answered him.

The rider removed a letter from his pouch. "I've orders to deliver this to the artist of that work." He pointed to the sculpture.

"That would be me." The artist reached out a hand for the letter.

The rider handed the letter to him. "It's from Sir James McCautry. It wasn't easy finding you."

"I suppose not." The artist pocketed the letter returning to his food.

"Aren't you going to read it? I can't leave without an answer, Sir."

The artist screwed up his face as he chewed. Giving a grumble of resistance, he opened the letter and read it. As he read, his face softened. He sent Benjamine to the hut for writing tools. When Benjamine returned, the artist scribbled a short note on the bottom of the page. He sealed the letter and handed it back to the rider. The artist sat back down. Finishing his meal, he watched the rider mount and disappear into the woods toward Eastereven.

The artist shook his head in sympathy. "That's the second time he's sent a messenger looking for the girl. I told him when he was here, she's gone, and I don't know that she's ever coming back." A wistful smile crossed the artist's lips. "He says he's uncontrollably drawn to this girl. I think he's in love with her. He wants to know if she's real. What do you think, Benjamine? Do you think she is real?"

Benjamine stopped gathering their utensils. "I don't know, Sir. I didn't really see her, so I can't honestly say."

The artist leaned back twirling a foot as if to generate his thoughts. "Ah, life is strange, Benjamine, strange and wonderfully interesting."

"Exciting and exhilarating," Benjamine added.

"Delightful. Absolutely delightful," the artist emphatically agreed.

19

Ida stroked her slender fingers through her long golden hair. She had been watching James for a long time, waiting for the opportunity to work her way into his life. In the past, they had met briefly during many social events. She failed to entertain his attention for long. Mary occupied too much of his time. His devotion to Mary was difficult for Ida to overcome.

In the last few weeks, Ida sensed a change in James's relationship to Mary. Although Mary had accompanied him to his estate in Eastham, Mary socialized with him less often. James spent most of his evenings with his friends at a popular tavern along Lake Knapp. Ida arranged through a mutual friend to join James. Gradually, James opened to Ida's advances of friendship. One evening, after drinking too much, he confided to Ida he felt something missing in his relationship with Mary. James blamed himself. Something was troubling him. What, he refused to say. Ida declined to invade his privacy. She deepened their friendship by lending a sympathetic ear and giving him her complete support.

The gesture paid well. James began to spend more time with Ida. He stole time in the afternoon hours to meet with her. They walked the shoreline of the lake while James unburdened himself of his feelings about Mary. Even though he admitted to Ida he felt he should end his relationship with Mary, he was reluctant to do so. Their talks strengthened their friendship. The effort wearied her to the extreme.

Ida inclined heavily against her dressing table. She handled her hairbrush in frustration. James and Mary were leaving for Yves in the morning. It might be months before James returned to his country estate in Eastham. As far as she was concerned, even a week was too long for them to be apart. James was only beginning to depend on their friendship for comfort. It would not take much to sever their new bond. Ida did not want to take the chance with a lengthy separation. She somehow had to take the initiative. Ida wrestled with her locks placing combs in her hair. She adjusted her dress, showing more of her shoulders than was necessary, and studied her image in the mirror. Satisfied, she ordered her carriage brought to the front door. She departed for the party unescorted.

When she arrived at the Tudman home, she casually mingled with the guests searching for a glimpse of James in the crowd. In anxious futility, an hour passed before she noticed Malcolm, a friend of James. She worked her way to his side chatting with the guests separating them. As she conversed with Malcolm, he informed her, "James and Mary were supposed to ride here with me. When I arrived they were having a disagreement. I expect they've canceled their plans for this evening." He lowered his voice in confidence, "I told him to come along without her when he got the chance. I even sent my coach back for him, but I don't think he'll come. Mary's very upset with James. She thinks he's spending too much time with you."

"We're only friends," Ida suppressed a smile.

"Oh, I know that. But you know how it is when two people are in love," Malcolm taunted her.

Ida flushed at his words. She felt herself burn with anger. Instinct cautioned her to take control. Ida excused herself. Finding private refuge in a room on the second floor, she paced the room venting her emotion, attempting to reorganize her thoughts. She decided to leave the party. Before she could carry out her decision, Malcolm sheepishly entered the room.

"I thought you might want to know. James is here. He's looking for you."

Ida thanked Malcolm, buoyant in her politeness. She walked with him to meet James. Noticing James was alone, Ida dared to greet him with a joyful, intimate embrace.

"Where is Mary?" she ventured with coyness.

"I left her at home." James displayed a hint of anger. His eyes spoke strongly to Ida's senses.

Ida called a servant to replenish his glass. As the evening pressed onward, Ida was gentle and cunning in her attentiveness toward James. She encouraged James in his excessive drinking. The more he drank, the more confident she felt about the outcome of the evening. Ida sent her coach home without her. She rode with James in Malcolm's coach. By the time they reached her Eastham estate, James succumbed to her petting. He insisted he walk her into the main house, waving Malcolm to leave as they approached the door.

In the morning, Ida boldly called a servant to her room requesting her private coach for James. The interruption made him uncomfortable. She soothed him by teasing him with her body, assuring him she could be trusted and pledging him her undying loyalty. When the coach was ready, she helped him dress and walked him to the coach. After he left, Ida ordered her servants to pack. She had decided to follow James to Yves.

Mary's heart sank when she saw Ida Eastham's carriage pull up to the front entrance of the estate house. She barely controlled the tears springing to her eyes as she saw James emerge. Her throat felt suffocating and tight. She greeted James pretending she hadn't seen the coach and tried to make amends for the previous evening. James easily responded to her arduous advances.

During the long ride to Yves, James became sullen. Mary quietly held his hand, avoiding his troubled stare. When they arrived at Yves, James buried himself in his work. After several days, he relaxed. He devoted more of his time to Mary. Mary dismissed the incident at Eastham as an unfortunate mistake. She vowed never again to allow another opening for female opportunism.

Ida sent a messenger ahead of her coach announcing her arrival at the Castle Yves. It was unusual for Lord Eastham's daughter to ignore the appropriate channels and, in an act of impulse, appear without her father for a prolonged stay. Although Sir Henry Caldwell was pleased Ida intended to spend the winter at the castle, her visit piqued Caldwell's curiosity. He strongly suspected she had set her affections on a member of the Court. Caldwell planned to insure her success with her suitor.

Ida's first act was to send James a note. Caldwell's servant Chad delivered it. When Mary saw Chad hand James the note, she cringed with instinctive defense. Upon learning its author was Ida, Mary locked herself in the bedroom, crying for several hours. After her tears, she insisted James ask Ida to leave the castle. He explained he could not make demands of Lord Eastham's daughter. To reject her would cause them both trouble at court. James begged Mary to let go of her jealousy and accept Ida as a friend. He assured her Ida would be content with their friendship. James's gentle reasoning and cooing voice temporarily soothed Mary's fears.

Within a week of her arrival, Ida received permission from Sir Henry Caldwell to attend James's musical sessions. She sat out of the way listening with delight. After the sessions, she held parties for the musicians. She remained gracious even on the few occasions when James declined her invitation to join her.

Boyden noticed Ida's hidden disappointment whenever James left her company to fulfill his obligations to Mary. At those times, he went out of his way to keep her company. His entertaining charm eased Ida's demure, while his affectionate bearing teased her sensitivity. The poetry in his mannerisms was sensual enough to pacify her romantic urgings for James.

Ida's presence remained unsettling to Mary. Her confident air was disturbing. Before long, Mary approached James requesting they hasten their marriage plans. James answered with painful clarity. He was not ready to marry. Before the week ended, Mary left Yves without bidding James good-bye. From Caldwell, James learned Mary's father had sent her home. Her position at court was quickly and quietly filled. With Mary gone, James fell into companionship with Ida.

Even with Ida's constant attention, the days waiting for the return of his messenger seemed to drag on endlessly. The foliage lost its soft color and the wind gathered its dried remains in the dusty gusts that blew across the castle grounds. By the time the hoofs of the messenger's horse beat furiously against the cool stones of the outer courtyard, James's eyes burned red with lack of sleep and his longing for the girl from the Arca V'ing Enta threatened to spill from the depths of his soul and drown him. When the messenger entered the music suite and handed him the letter, he could not control the trembling in his hands. As he opened it and hungrily read the scrawl from the artist's hand, his mind blurred. He played with the corners of the letter. As he blankly stared into space, he fought the emotions surging within him.

Rose saw the pain etching its way across his face. A sharp empathetic twinge darted from her senses to her heart. She reached out a hand toward him, and then drew back in hesitation. Reaching for her instrument, she blew a soft melody in compassion.

With a gaunt expression, James looked up at her. "I didn't hear you come in. Where are John and the others?"

Rose slowly removed the mouthpiece from her lips. "They'll be along soon, I'm sure. Are you all right?"

James, despondent, placed the letter in his pocket.

"Yes, I'm fine. When the others get here, tell them to start without me."

Without further explanation, James left the music suite. Rose sat for a moment affronted by his abrupt departure. Pouting, she opened the cabinet drawers and withdrew several music scores. She was laying the music out as John and the other musicians trickled into the room.

"Where is James?" John noted his absence.

"He said to start without him. I thought you'd like to start with this."

John looked over the pieces trying to unnerve Rose. "Seems fine to me," he agreed after a prolonged examination. Taking a flask of Grogg from his pocket, he settled into a chair. He took a drink from the flask and passed it amongst the musicians.

James heard the mingled sound of laughter and tuning instruments as he wandered the court gardens. The chill of the night air bit his face reminding him of his raw disappointment. He had been dreaming of her, longing for her, writing his songs for her since he saw her that day in Eastereven. Now, with the stark reality of the castle walls shadowing his footsteps and the mild tapping of the letter against his body, it seemed he had dreamed her after all.

The sound of activity from the music building interrupted his solitude, as he crossed from the lawns of the living quarters to the remote section of the property bordering the forest. As James walked, his sight focused on the stars brilliantly highlighting the crisp air. He sat in the grass watching the stars until the damp cold invaded his bones and the dry straw threatened to cut the skin of his hands. After trying to rub the sore imprint from his hands, he got up and made his way back to his music suite. When he returned to rehearsal, only Rose and John remained in his suite. Rose slept on the floor, her head sheltered with pillows.

"When you call a rehearsal you really should attend," John greeted him in a whisper.

"You're right," James admitted. He sat at the piano reviewing the sheet music, letting silence grow between them.

"It went well even without you. Ida came by. She was disappointed you weren't here."

James browsed through the music without purpose. "Are you too tired to listen to something I've written?"

"No, go ahead." John unclasped his guitar case. He pulled his chair closer to James.

As James played, John rested on his instrument. Before long, they were intimately involved with the new piece. They worked through the night battling each other in a creative exchange. Rose slept through their interchange.

In the morning, Rose awoke to find James asleep on a divan and John asleep in a chair. She looked over the music sheets recording their work. Rose stretched and yawned, ruffling her distraught hair as she studied the musical arrangement. She refrained from trying any notes on the piano. Looking about the room, she noticed James's coat flung haphazardly across the arm of the divan.

Her eyes glistened and her mouth crooked. She tiptoed past the sleeping gentlemen. With caution, she lifted the coat and moved her fingers along the inside of the coat with swift movement. Her fingers touched the letter James had placed in his pocket. She lifted the letter with a skillful hand, easing the coat back onto the divan. Sitting hidden in a corner behind a chair, she read the letter. As her eyes scanned the letter over and over, Rose drew in a deep breath. She returned the letter to James's coat pocket and lay on the floor digesting its words. "He isn't writing about Mary, or Ida. There is someone else." The thought surprised her. It gave her pleasure. As she drifted into sleep, Rose's youthful heart embraced the idea with romantic zest.

20

Ida felt an invisible threat silently invading the space between them. She didn't know who the threat was. She and James were developing an intimate and solid relation. There wasn't a visible sign James was interested in someone else, but Ida's acute intuition cautioned her otherwise. When James missed his rehearsal, Ida searched the castle and Altmont for him. He was nowhere to be found. She harbored her uneasiness, pacing the halls of Altmont, analyzing the significance of his absence. She wrestled with her imagined feelings of abandonment. Finding little relief in her aloneness, she wandered to Boyden's suite. Boyden comforted her distraught feelings. They talked through the night, disclosing their inner selves to each other. In the twilight of the morning, Boyden escorted her back to her room in the main castle.

Chad informed Henry Caldwell of Ida's distress with James. Chad felt certain James was not involved with anyone else. He had not left the compound since Ida arrived. It was reported James had sent a messenger to Eastereven, but the letters were addressed to an artist who lived along the Arca V'ing Enta. It was unlikely James met with another woman without Chad's contacts uncovering it. Caldwell was wary. His natural antagonism towards James fanned. He ordered Chad to keep a closer watch on James's activities at Yves. Lord Eastham's daughter must not suffer social embarrassment at the hands of an ambitious musician. Caldwell's anger simmered throughout the day. Lord Eastham had notified him of Ida's interest in James shortly after she had arrived at the castle. His daughter desired a lasting commitment with the titled musician. Lord Eastham approved of the match. He sequestered Caldwell's assistance in assuring his daughter's happiness.

After accepting Lord Eastham's request, Caldwell met with the Queen in private presenting an outline for Lord Eastham to increase his services for defense against Pilchard along the Epping Wall. Caldwell suggested Lord Eastham receive greater compensation for his services. Within his new proposal, he included an arrangement for the marriage of Ida to Sir James McCautry. The Queen was hesitant to include James in negotiations for Lord Eastham's services. Caldwell debated with her, until he finally swayed her his way. Caldwell called a meeting with Lord Pembroke to elicit his assistance in securing cooperation from James.

To Caldwell's surprise, Pembroke filled with resistance. "I can't ask him to do this."

"You're not asking him. The Queen is asking him. You're only negotiating the request."

"I don't expect him to agree to this."

"Well, why not? He's sleeping with the girl, isn't he? He should expect to marry her," Caldwell raised his voice infuriated.

"Marry her, maybe, but as part of a political arrangement? No, it's an insult. I can tell you right now he's done with this sort of thing."

"Pembroke, let me tell you, as long as he is a part of Yves, he won't be done with any of this," Caldwell shook with temper. "Lord Eastham won't have his daughter shamed or taken advantage of. That is a certainty. As long as Lord Eastham controls the forces along the Epping Wall, the Queen will support his wishes. Our job is to ensure Lord Eastham remains free from concern."

"You're worrying without cause. I'm sure he'll propose to her given his own time."

"Then it won't be a problem for him to make it official right now."

"And what about his other commitment," Pembroke dampened his voice, "to the Queen? Will that be brought to a close?"

"That will continue, of course." Caldwell's smile grated Pembroke. It scraped across the back of his neck like a cold poker and remained even after Caldwell ended their discussion and Willie prepared for the unpleasant task of telling James.

When James entered the darkened room, Pembroke was sitting alone in front of the fireplace watching the shadows cast by the flames. In the warmth of the firelight, his words flowed with ease. Pembroke spoke with conviction. His serious tone and resolve carried import and left James no room for argument. As James sipped his wine, he accepted the arrangement Pembroke offered him. Ignoring the underlying conflict within him, James assured Pembroke he supported the Queen's wishes for him to marry. At his words, Pembroke's confidence lagged. He stumbled on his words forming an apology.

"Willie, it's all right. I don't mind marrying her." James placed his empty glass down, rising to leave.

"You don't understand, James. I'm trying to tell you. You will be expected to continue your arrangement with the Queen as well." Pembroke's lip curled in helpless guilt.

James paled. Pembroke saw the crushing sorrow of defeat enveloping him. James stood, staring past Pembroke. Without speaking, he left. Pembroke, alone in the silence of the room, poured himself another glass of wine. His chest pressed with heaviness. As he drank, he felt certain the look on James's face would haunt him for some time to come.

Rose ran through the court gardens. Her heart beat furiously against her chest. Without knocking, she opened the door to James's rooms. Closing the door, she leaned her back against it. Her chest heaved with breathlessness.

James, startled by her abrupt entrance, lay down his pen. "What are you doing?" He bridled his sharpness.

Rose's nostrils flared. She cocked her head battling for composure. James waited, his eyebrows framing cautious irritation.

"You're going to marry her," Rose finally blurted out in fury.

James laughed. He turned back to his desk. "Yes, I'm going to marry her."

"You can't. You don't love her."

"The Queen plans to announce it at tomorrow's banquet."

Rose paced back and forth across the room trying to temper her frustration. Her volatile feelings bloomed into angry passion. Her hot breath fired the room. "You're selling out. I thought you were better than that."

"I don't know what you mean. I care for the girl. I'm marrying her. That's all."

"The girl in your songs... What about the girl in your songs?"

James laughed uneasily. "What do you mean, the girl in my songs? Rose, an artist imagines someone. Someone he's trying to reach, to touch. You see? It gives focus to the work."

"She's not Ida."

"She is anyone I say she is," James spit the words out in cold staccato.

"Then you're lying to yourself." Rose twisted her mouth with disgust.

"You don't know anything about this." James shook his head rankled.

"I know more than you think I do. I know you saw her at Eastereven," Rose sputtered in hasty retaliation. She heard James draw in an anxious breath.

"How do you know that?" His face reddened. His hushed intensity frightened Rose.

"I accidentally found your letter to the artist." Rose recoiled slightly as she spoke.

"You accidentally found it? Then you should know I imagined her."

"That's not what he said. He said he didn't know if she was ever coming back again," Rose countered.

"He's a crazy man, Rose. He lives in the deep part of the woods near the Arca V'ing Enta and creates the most unusual pieces you ever could imagine. But everyone seems to agree, his mind is not altogether in this world. No one else saw her, Rose, just he and I."

"You couldn't have imagined her if he saw her too."

"There is strong reason to suspect I did imagine her if he was the only other one who saw her. You can't let yourself get carried away by this idea about this girl. I've accepted it. I made an emotional error. Now, I've got to get on with my life." James picked up his pen tapping it against the desk.

"What about love?"

"What about it?"

"Your new songs are filled with such love and compassion. They touch me in a way no other songs ever have. I find it hard to believe you wrote them for someone who doesn't exist."

The stirring of a deep ache filled his eyes with tears. It smothered his heart. "Drop it, Rose," his thick tone warned her. He asked her to leave.

Rose pressed her ear against the closed door. She thought she heard him crying. Cussing herself with a closed fist, she dragged herself from his doorway. Her confrontation with him tickled her conscience. She was trying to help him, she justified. He was obviously confused.

When Rose overheard Henry Caldwell arranging his marriage, she felt certain James would strongly resist his authority, if only for a matter of principle. Instead, Rose had watched a deep sorrow overtake James, as the reality of spending his life with someone he didn't love burrowed its way into his soul. Her heart went out to him. It was simple to Rose. James needed help. Rose knew the Queen was sympathetic towards him. She didn't like to see him unhappy. She wondered if the Queen knew how the arrangement was affecting him. After confronting James about the marriage, she sent a messenger to the Queen requesting a private audience with her. She believed she could convince the Queen the arrangement was a personal coup by Caldwell to destroy James's happiness. Rose decided Pembroke would make a good ally presenting her case to the Queen. Under cover of night, she made her way to Pembroke's suite to enlist his assistance. Chad, accompanied by several guards, intercepted her in a deserted hallway.

"Lord Caldwell wants to see you." Chad's cool expression spurred Rose to try to run. The guards grabbed her and dragged her to Caldwell's receiving chamber.

"Rose, I'm quite upset with your behavior lately. You've gotten completely out of control." Caldwell stared viciously at her slight figure. Rose, in a casual manner, sat back in her chair. An unaffected expression decorated her face.

"You're always stirring up trouble for me. Now why would you want to see the Queen this evening? Should I guess or will you explain it to me?" Caldwell brandished the message Rose had dispatched to the main castle. " 'I feel Lord Caldwell has misled you concerning this arrangement between Sir James and Ida. It is adamant I speak with you this evening.' What is this all about? You're saying I intentionally misled her! You intended to accuse me of coercing the Queen? I will assume your accusations against me are a result of your youthful ignorance and lack of discipline."

Rose raised an eyebrow to him. She remained locked in silence.

"We were fortunate Chad intercepted this. I don't appreciate this. You intended to interfere in our affairs. You intended to interfere with the affairs of state in matters that affect the safety of Fiara. You are completely rebellious against my authority. Your overreactions are dangerous to me. Don't you know I could have you tried for treason for jeopardizing the defense of the Epping Wall?"

Rose felt a tightness grip her.

"It is only my fond affection for you as a ward of this court that allows me to overlook the problems you might have caused. But I see this as a serious warning. You need disciplining. These matters have always been left solely in my hands."

Without further explanation, Caldwell dismissed her. The guards led her through the back hallways to the bowels of the castle. As she descended into the musty darkness, her stomach churned. Even so, she maintained her confident air of defiance while the guards secured her legs and wrists to a cell wall and closed her into total darkness. Rose collapsed against the damp wall. As she felt the cold metal braces clamp down upon her skin, the darkness became unbearable.

Ida appeared stunning in her delicate ensemble. Her radiant appearance quelled James's heartfelt doubts. As the ceremony formalizing their engagement got underway, his spirits lifted, spurred by the festive celebration given by the court. The dancing, the laughter, the plentiful flow of drink dispelled his spiritual yearning. After the banquet, he searched the crowd hoping Rose had attended the ceremony. He admitted to Pembroke he was disappointed she had not.

Pembroke was not surprised by her stubbornness. "Sir Henry said she was very disappointed by your engagement. She needed time to herself. He suggested she leave for a holiday. I imagine there'll be many disappointed women in Fiara when they hear you are no longer available."

"Did he say where she went?"

"No, he didn't mention it. She may not want anyone to know."

When James approached Caldwell about her whereabouts, Caldwell hedged, "She is growing up, James. This holiday is all a part of growing up."

Weeks later, Rose reappeared within the bustle of castle life and resumed her activities in the Music Order. Without conferring with any of her friends, she moved from Altmont to a room in Caldwell's wing in the main castle and replaced her boyish outfits with traditional female dress. She attended only the musical rehearsals Caldwell scheduled for her. James felt she was avoiding him.

When their paths finally crossed, James asked with fond sensitivity, "What happened?"

Rose shrugged. "I grew up, I guess."

"Do you still want to rehearse with us?"

"I don't know." Rose lowered her eyes.

"You're welcome to join us whenever you'd like."

Rose looked up. "Thanks. I'll see." She brushed her skirt. "How do I look?"

"You're beautiful."

"Thank you." Rose hesitated. "See you." With grace, she moved down the hallway away from him.

As she disappeared from his sight, James's heart sank. He wondered how she could have changed so drastically in such a short time.

21

John erratically paced back and forth in his music suite fidgeting with his guitar. He was uncomfortable meeting with Bandore openly in his suite. John kept his activities with Bandore a secret, meeting with him as little as possible and then only in the darkened corners of the castle grounds. He disliked his character. Bandore reeked with the aura of disposed souls. He swaggered around the noblemen and musicians at court, heady with the power of a bully, carrying his disrespect like a bullwhip on his hip ready to snap and rip without mercy. Bandore knew when and where to strike his enemies, as well as his friends. He made little distinction between the two, depositing his venom with skilled marksmanship into their vital core. John disliked the man, but it was impossible to receive a personal supply of Grogg from Pilchard without contact with him.

John poured a glass of Grogg from the decanter he kept in his suite. As the first sip reached his mouth, he relaxed. The liquid soothed his jagged nerves. Over the last year, John had noticed a change in his desire for the drink. It was overpowering him.

Bandore arrived alone, entering the suite without knocking. With his hands clasped behind his back, he stalked the room several times before acknowledging John with his narrowed eyes, sneering lips and calculating bearing. When Bandore spoke, the tight pitch in his voice grated against John's senses. "We need some help from you to expand our influence in the world. I'm asking you, Boyden and other loyal supporters in the Orders to cooperate with our plans."

"What are we supposed to support?" John challenged.

"Grogg, John. You aren't stupid yet. Grogg. We plan on introducing Grogg to a larger audience. Bring it to the people. We should have done it long ago."

"Grogg isn't allowed outside of the Court."

"Pilchard and I decide where it is allowed. We don't need permission. We're bringing in a large shipment soon. It's better than what you're used to. We've decided to take it further than Yves. That's where we need you and the others."

"I thought that they limited the amount you could bring through the pass. The Eastham guards escort the transport from Pilchard to Yves. How are you going to get more Grogg past Lord Eastham and his men?"

"That's our problem, not yours," Bandore snapped.

"I'm not a peddler, Bandore. I'm a musician."

"You won't need to peddle anything. You won't have to do anything at all. Just see to it your share of the shipment and a few of my men travel with you and your musical group."

"How am I going to do that?"

"You're a creative man, John. You'll figure a way. We'll need space for several wagons."

John tugged at his lip with his fingers as he digested Bandore's request. "You make it sound simple. I can see problems with it."

"We're prepared for the problems, John," Bandore assured him with confidence. "Boyden and some of the others are scheduled to tour next week. If all goes well with them, we'll be ready for your part."

"We weren't planning to tour until summer."

"You'll have to change your plans. The most we can wait is a month. You'll volunteer to manage the entourage. You'll need to add a few key locations to your travel plan. Caldwell will agree to the changes. It will mean more revenue for him." Bandore poured John another drink of Grogg. He let the cap of the decanter fall to the floor. "I'll expect to keep in close touch with you from now on, but we'll keep it very quiet."

John watched the decanter cap roll in swoops along the floor. Bandore laughed as it settled against the leg of a chair. When John looked up at him, Bandore shook his head and left.

"The plans have been changed," John said as he entered the rehearsal hall late one evening. "We're touring next month."

"What do you mean, next month?" James stopped playing.

"Caldwell has changed the schedule. We go out next month."

"Are you sure?"

"I talked with him today. I agreed to the change for us. I hope you don't mind."

James pulled at his earlobe, furrowing his brow. "No. I guess not. I planned on the summer, though. I don't know if we'll be ready for a spring tour."

"We're almost ready now." John assured him. "We won't need more than a month to pull our act together."

James nodded with depressed surrender. "You're probably right. I suppose it doesn't matter when we go, as long as we go."

John stiffened his pose. He looked at him and noticed the weariness overtaking James like an insidious disease. The charming sparkle in his eyes had dulled. A blanket of heaviness subdued his charismatic manners. John, at first, had tried to cover his absent stares and lack of concentration at court functions with his own sharp, witty responses; but it became increasingly obvious to everyone that James was troubled. By rote, he moved through the activities of the Order. Fearful of ridicule, James refused to discuss his feelings with his friend. John grew testy and impatient with him, flaying James in temper to rouse him from his vague complacency. Frustrated, John finally gave in with reluctance, accepting his new persona as permanent. He repressed his sense of kinship to him and his compassion for his friend cooled. On occasion, John was touched by the pained look in his eyes or the sound of hopelessness in his voice. Then John would say in a quiet voice, as he did now, "If I knew how, I'd help lift you're spirit."

James winced, crinkling the corners of his eyes at John's perception. For a moment, he thought John knew about the girl. Perhaps Rose had told him about the letter, or perhaps John had somehow sensed the mushrooming desire for her pulsing through his heart every moment of every day. He couldn't seem to forget her, no matter how hard he tried to push the tenderness and love away. His feelings constantly tore at him beneath the surface of his façade. It didn't make any sense to him—made him feel crazy. He had only seen her once, for a few brief moments imagined her.

Trying to hide his feelings from John, James laughed and asked, "When do we do the schedule?"

"It's done. Caldwell took care of it already. I have it here if you want to take a look." John pulled the paper from his pocket.

As he smoothed it out, James looked over his shoulder at it. "This is grueling. We'll be out for months. Why are we playing such a long tour?"

"Caldwell says, revenue, my dear boy." John pinched his nose as he imitated the Lord Advisor for the Arts. "Caldwell is pleased for our generous contribution to the treasury. No one will keep him from his noble purpose."

James broke into uncontrollable laughter as he continued down the list of sites for their tour. When his eyes rested on the name of the last scheduled site, a thrill quickened within him. "Eastereven," he whispered.

Pleasure lit John's face. "That was my idea, James. It's a long ways, but I know the area inspires you."

The thought of Eastereven sparked James. He tackled the tasks of preparing for the tour with renewed energy and enthusiasm. His desire to perform grew stronger each day. In restless fervor, he worked long hours, aching with anticipation for the journey. Before the end of the month, they were ready to tour.

Boyden and his group returned to Yves under the laurels of a successful tour. Several days later he visited John in his suite. It was late. John, preparing to retire for the night, met him with annoyance. "Can't it wait? I need some sleep."

"No, it can't wait. We need to talk." Boyden, brushing past him, sat down burying his face in his hands. With despair, he raised his eyes searching for John.

"Do you realize what he's gotten us into? We're spreading Grogg across the face of Fiara."

"Don't be so dramatic. We're carrying extra Grogg. We always carry Grogg."

"That was before. Now we're not just carrying Grogg. At each engagement, his men set up for refreshments, our complements, of course. The people loved it. You and I know how easy it is to love the stuff. If I understand this plan, by the end of this season a great deal of people in Fiara will want

Grogg. Especially if you take it all the way to Eastereven with your tour." Boyden wriggled his foot with his mounting anger.

"I thought that was the idea."

"John, think about what we're doing. We're not just buying Grogg here for our personal use or sharing it with a few friends. We're transporting the stuff to areas in which it's forbidden. We're actually working for Pilchard. It's much worse than that. I think this is only part of a greater plan, more than just increasing his market. And his men are distributing the Grogg using us as a guise. It's free with our compliments. Not Pilchard's complements, not Bandore's, ours. They are publicly making us the guilty party. That's what the Queen will think, when word of its spread reaches her. And eventually it will. It may take some time, but it's inevitable." Boyden felt a tight pressure squeeze along his temples and the back of his neck waiting for John to speak.

As tension filled the room, a click of the door disrupted the silence. Bandore narrowly eyed Boyden. "You've been avoiding me, Boyd. I don't like that."

Boyden squirmed, flushing under Bandore's hot stare. He picked at the cloth along the arm of his chair. Bandore closed the door and circled Boyden, his ire reflecting with every step. "You're having doubts. You should keep them to yourself."

"I've done what you asked. You don't have any reason to complain."

"Yes," Bandore hissed. He tightened his lips as he rubbed the bridge of his nose. "What about the next time?"

"Don't ask me for more." Boyden flicked his fingers along the arm chair. He got to his feet and left.

John's stomach tightened at the sound of the closing door. Bandore lifted his eyes to him.

"Nothing has changed," John answered, a hoarseness abrading his throat.

Bandore's eyes shifted back to the door. A chuckle escaped his curling lips.

Boyden wandered the empty hallways of Altmont. Edginess spiked him within the deep quiet of the night. After resting a few moments in a deserted practice room, uneasiness overcame him once again. He walked to the reception area where the night clerk and several watchman assigned to the building had gathered. Sharing a warm drink, he sat with them, passing the night in friendly conversation. When daybreak lit the building with its gray light, he returned to his suite. Without undressing, he fell onto the bed and went to sleep.

In early evening, he awoke. He bathed, dressed and took dinner in the dining room with the other members of his musical group. After dinner, he visited James and John at rehearsal.

"It sounds good," Boyden commented during a break. "Why don't you come by tonight when you're done here and have a few drinks?"

"We can't," James explained with apology. We have to rework an arrangement by tomorrow. John and I will be up most of the night working on it."

When they began to play again, Boyden left the rehearsal. In his suite, he lay down, tossing and turning against a veil of sleep. Unable to surrender to rest, Boyden rose. After changing his shirt, he made his way to the main castle and Ida's private rooms. He shuffled his feet waiting for her to answer his knock on the door.

"James is working all night. I thought you might like some company," he offered when she opened the door.

Ida giggled in sensual release. She led him into her receiving room. Petting his shoulders in fondness, she removed his jacket. She went to a locked cupboard hidden behind a utility shelf, removed a small decanter of Grogg, and poured them each a glass. When Boyden took a seat she sat close to him. They slowly sipped the Grogg, playfully stirring each other's passion. Before long, Ida unbuttoned Boyden's shirt and found refuge in the bare warmth of his well-defined muscles.

Boyden lovingly caressed Ida's cheek as she slept. He loved the evenings they spent together, moments stolen when James buried himself in his work. He believed Ida had been hasty in her choice. No one could love her quite as much as he did. Boyden laid his lips on her forehead. Gently, he released his embrace. With caution, he disentangled his clothing from the bedcovers. In the receiving room, he gathered his shirt and jacket and dressed. He hesitated in leaving.

Boyden again slept through the day, missing a morning rehearsal and several production meetings. He awoke in late afternoon with Ida's scent lingering in his memory. Gazing toward the light filtering through the windows of his room, he drifted back to sleep still feeling her soft body ebbing within his dreams.

A harsh knocking on the suite door intruded upon his satisfying slumber. When he opened the door, the Royal Guards directed their weapons at him. Without explanation, several guards took hold of him, placing him in heavy chains. Ignoring his heated and frightened questioning, they forced him through the music building, across the castle grounds and into the dark confines of the lower prison. Inside the prison, he was chained to a cell wall and abandoned.

It seemed like hours before the heavy door cracked open and the shadowy figure of Henry Caldwell entered the cramped space of the cubicle. "You're in a lot of trouble, Boyden." Caldwell wrinkled his nose in distaste.

Boyden caught his breath. The color drained from his face. He held his tongue, waiting for Caldwell to accuse him of treason.

Caldwell sighed, shaking his head. "I don't like to see you in here. You're one of the best I have. I can't afford to lose you, but it doesn't look good. The evidence is overwhelming."

Boyden felt a pinched weakness pass through him. He tried to control his breath as he asked, "What am I accused of?"

Henry Caldwell paused, examining Boyden with critical eye. "Lord Chaffee's daughter has disappeared. He believes she has been harmed, and he has accused you of the crime."

"I'd never harm anyone. You know that," Boyden balked with surprise and relief.

"The evidence says otherwise. There appears to have been a struggle. Anna was your lover, wasn't she?"

"I wouldn't say that," Boyden defended himself.

"We would," Caldwell cut the air with his sureness.

"Where were you last night? We know you were in the castle."

Boyden, with obstinate melancholy, held back an answer.

Caldwell scrutinized him without pressing him further. "Lord Chaffee is furious. He wants you interrogated. I'm holding him off for now. If she doesn't turn up alive soon, they'll insist on questioning you. You know what that means. It won't be pleasant." Looking around the cell, a shudder passed through Caldwell. "I'll do my best to help you." Caldwell stepped outside the cell, allowing the guard to enclose Boyden within its desolation.

Caldwell stared out the window into the clear night sky. A cool draft pushed its way through the edges of the window into his study. The chill he carried from the prison grew stronger with the wafting of the night breeze. He called on Chad to bring him a warm drink. As he sipped the drink, he sifted through the evidence against Boyden. "Hysterical accusations," he thought. "She could have left on her own."

Caldwell wanted to dismiss the accusations against Boyden, but a witness had come forth claiming he had seen Boyden entering Anna Chaffee's room the evening of her disappearance. There were signs of a violent struggle in her bedroom. The witness could have been mistaken. He swore he was not.

Other than the struggle, there were no signs of fowl play. Boyden, dressed for a lady, had been seen leaving Altmont by the night clerk. A watchman reported Boyden had returned by a back entrance about daybreak. A lovers' quarrel, perhaps, Sir Henry surmised; or a tantrum contrived by a spoiled nobleman's daughter. Without a body, Caldwell felt it premature to assume Anna had been harmed. In his distraught rage, Lord Chaffee did not agree with him. If Anna was not found by the end of the week, Lord Chaffee would appeal for formal charges against Boyden. Though Caldwell felt the evidence against Boyden was weak, he had seen others in Fiara convicted on less. To ensure an unbiased investigation, Caldwell planned to assist in its every phase. In the morning, he intended to question the witness himself. When Caldwell was sure all the facts were collected, he would talk with Boyden again.

It was late evening before Ida heard Boyden had been imprisoned, accused in the disappearance of Anna Chaffee. Ida tried to leave Yves to find James. A curfew had been enforced on the compound. She was not allowed to leave the main castle until morning. Ida's mind swirled in confused thought. Boyden had been with her the evening Anna had disappeared, yet no one had questioned her. He must be waiting for the investigation to clear him, protecting her from social humiliation. Ida warmed at the thought of his chivalry. To vindicate him, she would have to publicly admit her infidelity. She cringed at the consequences of coming forward with the truth. It would be so much easier for her if she could wait to see if Anna turned up alive and well.

A coldness knifed through her when she thought of Boyden imprisoned in the bleak darkness of the lower prison. As her feelings for him tore against her fear, her conscience grew until she became anxious and desperate. In the middle of the night, she hurried to Caldwell's chambers.

"I need to speak to Sir Henry," Ida informed Chad when he answered her furious knocking.

"He's sleeping. It will have to wait for morning."

"I need to speak with him now," she called against the closing door. One of the castle guards, hearing her protests, advanced towards her, herding her back through the hallways to her room.

Ida, dazed, dressed for bed. Her mind clouded with thoughts of Boyden. As the night wore on, she dozed. When morning light filled her room, she washed and dressed to face Caldwell. She was placing a finishing touch to her hair when James let himself into her room.

"I can't talk now. I have to meet with Sir Henry," Ida dismissed him with rough briskness.

"Ida," he called her name softly. "Boyden took poison sometime in the night."

Ida's hands started shaking. "He was in prison. How could he get poison?"

"He must have been carrying it with him. Somehow he managed to take it."

Ida trembled uncontrolled. James gathered her into his arms. He held her close, kissing her; but her distress would not ease.

John sat quietly in the rehearsal hall, waiting for James to return to Altmont. The hush of the empty hall mirrored the sorrow filling his heart. His eyes stared past the broken guitar string he twirled between his fingers. Bandore's noisy footsteps echoed through the hall. His craggy voice ripped the air.

A smile crept stealthily along Bandore's lips when he saw John's lone figure bandied against him. John's unbending silence reeked with accusation. His wounds lay open. Bandore relished the moment intensely, walking arrogantly back and forth in front of John before turning to him. "It's too bad about Boyden." He clicked his tongue slowly three times and laughed when John blanched. "Makes it look like he's guilty. That's the conclusion they'll come to eventually, you know."

John glared at Bandore, disdain glinting in his eyes. He remained silent.

Bandore starkly returned John's look with steeled assurance. "It's too bad, for Boyden. Be careful you don't suffer the same fate." Bandore turned and walked back through the hall, his steps reverberating against John's solitude.

22

Even as James rummaged through the closet his vacant feelings stung him like a continuous undercurrent, reminding him of the sorrowful events of the week. The remains of Boyden, wrapped in a soiled shroud from the prison, had lain in the dirt as the gravediggers shoveled the ground to make a hole. A light mist drizzled, cold against his face, as he watched the dirt spatter against the smudged cloth. He saw the men grasp the edges of the shroud, dragging it to the edge of the grave. With a shove, it rolled, disappearing from sight.

Ida broke down and cried, pressing her face into his chest. He held her, supporting her quivering body. As the shovels pushed the mound of dirt into the grave, she tore away from his arms, swaggering in her grief across the back lot toward the castle. James looked at John. John wiped the rain collecting on his face with the palm of his hand. The gray image lingered, refusing to fade into the recess of his mind.

James lay his clothing onto the bed, despondency invading the hollow feeling within him. He moved into the depths of the closet. Stumbling, his foot kicked against his knapsack. He reached down, pulling it into the light of the room. James squatted, searching the inner pockets of the sack until his fingers finally touched the crystal wing. Withdrawing it from the knapsack, he held it firmly within his fist in relief. He had almost forgotten it. Since returning from Eastereven, it had lain hidden in his closet with his knapsack. He had forgotten to take it with him to Eastham and had ignored it when he returned. The memory of using it, made him feel uncomfortable, unsettled, and made it difficult for him to live with the routine of his world. The wing carried him outside of the world. It separated him from the normal, the expected, and seemed to drive him away from his ambitions, forcing him to see in a new light. Still, he hesitated, returning the wing to the knapsack. He withdrew it again and placed it around his neck.

James busied himself with packing for the tour. As he closed the lid to one of his trunks, a strong pull gripped the inside of his body. He rested his forearms along the top of the trunk resisting sleep. Recovering in weakness, he went to the closet, fumbling for a pair of his shoes. Lightheadedness overcame him. An image of a crystal wing splashed across the darkness of the closet. Hands reached for the wing. As James strained to see who held the wing, a light blinded him. Grabbing his forehead, he dropped his shoes and slumped onto the floor.

When he awoke, the glow of a lamp highlighted the floor. The rich sound of a gentle song mellowed the air. He lifted himself to his knees. A bed covered with a pastel floral spread blocked his side. A young woman, her back towards him, brushed her hair aside with her hand. Her head bowed for a moment before she slowly turned towards him. When her face became visible, he recognized her.

"It's you."

Erin's eyes lifted to James in surprise. She released the crystal wing from her fingers, her song broken. Warmth filled her eyes as she recognized him.

James checked his excitement. "You were at the ball at Eastereven."

"Yes, I was." Erin blushed.

"I tried to find you. I thought I had dreamed you."

"No, I was there. Why were you looking for me?"

"I wanted to meet you." James's voice grew husky, "What's your name?"

"Erin."

James tenderly reached for her hand. "I'm James." As his hand touched hers, it passed through her. James drew back startled. "You are a dream."

"No, I'm not." Erin lifted the crystal wing from her bosom holding it out for him to see. "I think it has to do with this. I think you are here with me in spirit."

"Am I dead?"

"No, you're not dead."

"Then I'm dreaming."

"No." Her eyes captured his. James looked deep into their softness, longing to melt into her in intimacy. He settled onto the floor with her, soft with the fullness of his blossoming love.

Erin told him of Venoma and the history of the crystal wings. She described her visit from the Lady of the Sun and her excursion to the Jewel of Light. As she spoke, she began to realize how important this man was to her, how familiar to her being, how connected she felt. It was more than the crystal wings. She stopped speaking, looking deeply into his eyes. James began to tell her of his life in Fiara. He revealed his chance meeting with the old man and began to disclose his deepest feelings and his pain. As he spoke, he touched upon an inner light he had never known. Without warning, he awoke on the floor of his closet. His heart beat with violence, his breath came in deep gulps, and his body felt unbearable, heavy.

James struggled to his feet, his head throbbing with the incessant knocking on his door. He slipped the crystal wing over his head and into his shirt pocket as he made his way to the door.

Ida grazed past him into the room. "You're not even ready yet," she fumed. "I've been waiting dinner for you in my rooms."

"I'm sorry. I forgot. I was packing."

Ida moved close to him in affection, running her hand along the nape of his neck. "Come along. You need to eat something."

"I'm not hungry."

"Then sit with me while I dine."

Ida poured herself a drink while James went into the bedroom to change. When James finished changing his clothes, he placed the crystal wing into the pocket of his dinner garb before leaving the bedroom to join Ida. As they dined within the soft light of candles, James picked absently at his food. The rhythm of Ida's idle conversation droned in his ears, humming in senselessness, until it seemed to carry him back through the Arca V'ing Enta to the memory of Erin.

From the first day he found Erin, his spirit lifted. He began to use the crystal wing again and again to visit her. James wanted to share her life as much as possible, even though he knew that their worlds were like ghosts to each other. He was overcome with love, a love that ran true within the core of his being. The love in him created a brilliant and warm energy that constantly swelled within his being; his eyes sparkled, his every step was buoyant, his every movement was graced with confidence and charm.

John was thrilled with the change in his partner. He realized it was more than an eagerness to return to Eastereven. His friend was in love. John was not the only one who noticed it. It was not long before the entire court buzzed with the news of his change in heart. James was in love. He had finally fallen in love with Ida. Ida wore the rumors like a trophy. She didn't care if it wasn't true.

As they finished the preparations for their tour, John once again began to feel bonded to his friend. James, shining with the open innocence of love, reminded John of the young man he had first encountered years ago along the dusty trails leading from the village of Poule toward Lake Tazia. That young man had a bright innocence that touched John's cynical and worldly heart right from the start. The young James had melted John's rugged character, hewn by the struggles of his poverty, with his sweet, sentimental love songs and his romantic visions of life. His enthusiasm solidified John's own dreams of success and made them seem real. John loved that young man like a brother. The memories moved him, stirred his old loyalty. He could feel their connection strengthening with every day that drew them closer to the first concert.

When the tour began, their chemistry had once again become magnetic. The songs flowed easily one into another, syncopating the air with their distinctive rhythms. Their own energy pulsed within the structure of the songs, charging the audience with excitement. The exchange was vibrant and constant, culminating to peak in frenzy. James and John savored each moment. They took their bows with enthusiasm, invigorated and renewed by each audience.

The entourage drove further into the southern regions of Fiara. At every engagement, they validated their worth to the royal court. The crowds were enormous. Their popularity was astounding, seeping them with the heat of notoriety and the headiness of success. James took it with peaceful stride. His thoughts always strayed beyond the audience to the Arca V'ing Enta and the young woman. He never noticed Bandore's men in their subtle maneuvers through the crowds. After each performance, he hurried away from the troupe. In his bed, he lay quiet allowing the crystal wing around his neck to carry him to Erin. In Venoma, James walked Erin through his life. He shared his pain and his hopes, opening his inner self to her soul. With each meeting, his yearning for her grew even stronger, until he could not imagine himself without her company.

At Alton, the entourage camped in a field owned by the Queen, a planned resting place before making a northwestern swing towards Sumatra. A steamy mist slithered along the low hills near the camp, eerie tentacles from the bogs lying on their fringe. Dusk filtered the horizon with a swarthy haze. Dank chill bit the air with a marshy aroma. Foreboding restlessness gnawed at James as they rode through the campsite. A strange choice for respite, he thought. He tethered his mount, transferring his pack to his tent. As the crew finished settling the area, James surveyed their activity, the raw, crisp dampness invading him. John soon noted his unusual watchfulness. He steered James away from the hurried movements of the men, distracting his vigilance with conversation, until the cooks announced mealtime. James nibbled at the food scooped in abundance onto his plate. His appetite waned with each bite. Without finishing, he left John and returned to his tent. Blanketed by the night, he slipped the crystal wing from his pocket and over his head.

When he awoke, burdened with physical discomfort, he lay listening to the stillness in the camp. Through the quiet, he heard the sounds of a rider. Muffled snatches of conversation floated across the grounds. Removing the crystal wing from around his neck, he placed it into the inner pocket of his shirt, buttoning the pocket as he got up. With caution, he moved closer to the source of the voices. From his hiding place, he could hear a muffled conversation. The transport had arrived. It was hidden and ready for transfer. James, remaining hidden, followed the men along a fog covered path leading to a small cave nestled in a hillside. Concealed by the fog, James hid in the brush near the cave. He waited, prostrate on the wet ground as the men entered the tight mouth of the cave. When the men emerged, the rider directed them to drive a wagon each night to the foot of the path. His men would carry the Grogg by hand from the cave to the wagon. When the men from the camp agreed to his terms, the rider led them back down the hillside.

James lingered until they were out of site before rising from his hiding place to follow them. A noise from the cave forced him to dig back into the brush for cover. He lay in the dampness, watching as several men dressed in black clothing squeezed through the cave opening and sat down outside the mouth of the cave.

"It's good to breathe some fresh air again," one of the men chided. "I'm beginning to feel like a mole after that trip."

"It's a long way to travel underground," another added. "It's the first time that's difficult. At least, the tunnels are wide enough for carts. Pilchard would have us carry the stuff on our backs if they weren't."

"Go on. I wouldn't do it," another protested.

"You'd do it all right, or Pilchard would end you. These natural tunnels are the only way to get it into Fiara while Lord Eastham camps along the Epping Wall. Finding them was worth the time and effort exploring our gruesome land. With these tours, we've gained a lot of ground."

"It'll be good when we're a part of the outside world again," another commented.

"I think the outside world will soon be a part of us," one laughed.

A light snapping of twigs brought the men to their feet. James crouched, afraid. He was relieved when the rider appeared through the fog. "Get back inside," he snarled to the men.

"No one can find us here," one of the men objected.

"There are only a few of these openings. We're not to take chances. Where are the others?" the rider barked.

"They are in the lower tunnel."

"Then you join them," he ordered the man. "The rest of you will stay with me inside the mouth. We'll guard the opening."

The men squeezed into the cave through the opening, one by one. When the last one disappeared, James crossed the land leading down the hillside. Before he could reach the path, men rapidly bolted through the mouth of the cave. They descended upon him, overpowering him with merciless brutality. When his body lay still, they dragged him through the mouth of the cave into the tunnel below.

23

"McCautry, McCautry!" the voice cawed echoing fiercely with an irritating nasal pitch disturbing James's fitful sleep.

"What now?" he thought and rolled over on the rocky ground, avoiding an inevitable confrontation with his tormentor. Through a mental cloud he heard the scuffling of feet moving along the outside corridor and entering the room. He felt someone hovering dangerously close. In defiance, he ignored him. An acute pain traveled across his back through his ribcage as a foot jarred a bruised area of his body.

"Will you leave me alone?" James lashed out in anger, dragging himself to a sitting position to nurse himself.

"We don't have to beat you again. It's obvious you know too much. Max was waiting for me to decide what's to be done with you. Max wants to keep you alive. I don't. Max presented me with good reasons to keep you alive, but," Bandore turned to his companion with a twisted smile of triumph. "I could have told you what I would decide, right Max? I told you now, didn't I?"

"Yes, you certainly did." Max looked away with light disgust. "You're not giving him a chance. At least give him a chance."

Bandore glared at Max. Max, unmoved by his intimidation, concentrated on James. "Bandore could wait to execute you. Pilchard isn't here right now. When he returns, Bandore could tell him you can be trusted to work with us. If you were willing to do that, Pilchard might spare you."

"I can't do that." James squinted, his fear threatening to overtake him.

"He needs time to think about it." Max looked over his shoulder at Bandore.

"He doesn't have any time. We'll execute him as soon as I decide how it will be done. He can think about that, Max."

With sullen resignation, Max watched Bandore huff out of the chamber. He stared into empty space and shook his head, heaving a light sigh. "Well, I guess we could clean you up a bit and give you a decent meal for a change."

Max helped James to his feet. He supported his weakened body as he walked him through the narrow cavern passageway and up a natural rock stairwell into another dryer cell. Max guided James through the entrance, laying him on a stone shelf padded with makeshift bedding. He ladled him a cup of water from a bucket on the floor. After James sipped some water,

Max cleaned his cuts and bruises with a solution from a kit kept on the small wooden table gracing the center of the cramped room. When he finished, he ordered a guard to bring James a meal.

"After you've eaten, I'll take you to one of the bathing springs. There's one close by."

James, nodding, lay back into the bedding seeking comfort. Cold from the rock surface seeped its way through the bedding chilling him. The hard stone heightened the painful sensations stabbing through his bruised body. He lay quiet, his eyes burning under puffy lids, stubbornly resisting the urge to groan. When his dinner arrived, he dragged himself over to the table. With gratitude, he devoured the soft foods garnishing the plate.

"Bandore's news hasn't affected your appetite," Max laughed as James mopped the plate with a chunk of bread, gathering the last juices into his mouth.

"I'm hungry. You've hardly fed me." James reached for a cup of water Max offered him. He lowered his eyes. "How long, Max? How long will it be before Bandore decides?"

"He'll make you wait. He likes his victims to squirm. I'm sure you sensed that."

"And you're not like that."

"I can be, but not this time. I like you, James. I appreciate your creativity. I think it's a shame to destroy someone like you. It's too bad you got caught up in all this." Max saw his words infiltrate James. He sensed a feeling of hopelessness crush him. Max leaned in close to him. "You could consider my suggestion. I'm sure I can stall Bandore, if you do."

"I can't betray the Queen." James's eyes moistened with strain.

Max sat back with repugnance. "Why, I've never seen such loyalty! Perhaps the Queen is not worthy of your loyalty. You don't know her like I do. She has a dark side. I've seen her sentence the innocent with the guilty and never think about separating the two. And she has dark moods. They keep her awake at night." Max brandished a fist, his face scowling. He kicked the dust as he spoke. "I should know. I used to fix her a potion, every now and then to help her sleep. One night, one of my mixtures seems to have made her ill. She accused me of trying to poison her. Poison her. That's when I decided to join Pilchard. I hadn't much of a choice." Max relaxed his fists. He opened his hands to James. "You see. One really isn't all that different from the other. You give your loyalty blindly, as if you owe her. The truth is she needs you. You are very popular with the people. You are politically valuable, both to her and to us. Power in this world, James, is an illusion. Its balance is very delicate." Max fixed his gaze on James. He folded his arms. "It's a waste for you to die. It won't help anyone. Not you. Not us. Not the Queen."

"I won't betray the Queen," James said in a thin voice. He looked away from Max's harsh face.

"So you won't betray the Queen." Max unfolded his arms. He tapped James's arm. "Come on, then. I'll take you to the baths."

Max grabbed a blanket from the bedding and a torch from the wall. He led James through a darkened tunnel to a chamber housing an underground pool. Max sat on the rocks bordering the entrance to the chamber. Holding the torch high, he watched its light shimmer across the water far below him. He directed James to walk down to the edge alone.

At the spring's edge, James hesitated to disrobe. "I can't see a thing. It is dark like pitch down here."

"Don't worry. The water is fresh and clean. We don't use this one much. There are others in the tunnels closer to the surface."

Max secured the torch while James removed his clothing. When he had submerged in the waters, Max walked to the pool's edge, handing him a soft bar of soap. "Here. Use this to clean yourself."

After James took the bar, Max settled on the ledge at the edge of the pool. The sound of water cut into the darkness.

"It's deadly quiet down here, isn't it?" Max's face, shadowed by the dim light of the torch, squinted looking towards James. Unable to clearly see him, Max changed his gaze to vacant space. "I don't like it down here. It's stuffy."

"Bleak," James offered.

"That's a good word. No, it's much worse than bleak." As James climbed out of the pool, Max tossed him the blanket. "Use this to dry off. And don't bother with your clothes. They're filthy. The guards should have something for you to wear by the time we get back there. Use the blanket for cover on the way back."

"I'd rather keep my own clothes." James nervously picked up his shirt feeling for the wing in its pocket. "I can wash them here before I go back." James deftly unbuttoned the shirt pocket. Sheltering himself within the dark beyond the torch light, he slipped the wing over his head, covering himself and the wing with the blanket.

"Don't bother." Max took the torch in hand and approached James. "They won't dry in time. Come on. I'll take you back." Max removed the clothing from James's hands. He pressed him forward through the long tunnel and back into the stone cell. James weakly sidled onto a chair, resisting the constant sensations of faintness that surged through him.

"I could use some clothes. This blanket is wet," James softly reminded Max, his eyes rolling with his deep breaths in his waning effort to remain conscious.

Max laughed and called a guard into the cell. He handed him the clothing. When the guard left the room, Max removed a flask from the floor and filled a cup, pushing it toward James. "You look uncomfortable. Drink this. It will help with the pain."

James empathically refused. "No. I want my head clear."

"I wouldn't if I were you." Max tried to coax James to drink the liquid. He was interrupted when a guard entered the cell with clothes for James. Max turned his back while James struggled to dress himself. When he finished, the crystal wing lay hidden from sight under his shirt. He wearily tossed the blanket over the chair and slumped onto the edge of the hard bed.

"Will you be staying with me right along?" he asked Max, his tongue slurring with heaviness and fatigue.

"Yes. I'll stay to the bitter end. Bandore wants someone with you every moment."

"Would you do me a favor then? I have a last request?"

"I don't know, James," Max shook his head.

"I need some time to myself. I need to be alone. If you would give me some time alone, I'd appreciate it."

Max bent his head in thought. "It seems reasonable to me. There's no way for you to escape from down here. I'm sure Bandore wouldn't approve of indulging your whims, but that's all the more reason for me to do it."

"Thanks, Max," James managed as severe fatigue gripped through his body. As Max left the cell, James laid himself carefully onto the rock bed. As he lay on his stomach in the dim light of the cell, the image of a wing flashed and dissolved. A stabbing pain spread through his head. He spun into unconsciousness.

James pulled himself to his knees and looked deeply into Erin's eyes. She held a hand out to him. He placed his hand along hers.

"I've been so worried about you." Erin's eyes moistened with tears. A weight pressured the inside of her chest.

"I had to see you one more time. I need to tell you." James moved his fingers gently tracing her cheekbone as if touching her. "I love you," he whispered, filling with sorrow.

"I love you, too." Erin felt a tear roll along her face.

His eyes filled with agony. "I haven't much time. Pilchard's men are going to kill me. I just wanted you to know I love you. I wanted to say good-bye."

"No!" James heard Erin's voice shriek. It echoed with violence through his head. His body shook with its resonating tone. James lifted his head to Max's touch. Max released his shoulder.

"Get him up," Bandore barked with impatience.

Max dragged James to a sitting position. James steadied himself on the edge of the bed, his body felt heavy. He struggled to get his breath.

"It's poison, James. I've decided on poison," Bandore informed James with a matter-of-fact air. "Max, you mix and give it. I'll want to watch."

"When do you want it?" Max raised his brows.

"Soon," Bandore snapped at him. Turning to James, he smiled, and then scurried out of the cell.

James covered his face with his hands. "Well, that's that."

His sarcasm touched Max. He drew closer to him. "Look, tell him you're willing to work with us. It would buy you some time. I don't know how much, but it would buy you some time."

"Max, I told you I can't do that."

"Then you lose, my friend. And I must say, I'm sorry for that."

A few moments later, Bandore returned to the cell and ordered Max to mix the poison. "We'll give it to him right here. There's no sense in moving him. It won't take long."

When Max left for his workroom, Bandore went with him, leaving several guards outside James's door. Alone in the cell, James ran his fingers along the inside wall of the chamber. Over the rock shelf serving as his bed, he found a rock loose enough to pry and remove. He frantically deepened the small opening until he could fit the wing safely inside, entombing it with the rock. With the crystal wing secured from his captors, James sat at the table waiting for their return. When they returned to the cell, Max carried a cup in his hand. He placed the cup on the table in front of James.

"Come on. Drink up," Bandore squawked. "I want you gone."

James stared at the cup without moving. "What's it going to be like?" The words barely escaped his parched throat.

"I tried my best to mix it well," Max comforted him, "but I'm afraid it will still be unpleasant."

James smiled meekly. "My hands are shaking."

"Come on. Come on. Don't waste our time," Bandore pressured him.

"Why don't you leave us alone?"

"I don't trust you, Max. That's why. Now drink up. I guarantee your second choice will be much worse than this."

Max roughly grasped the back of James's head, positioning the cup between his lips. "Drink it fast, all right? Ready?" James closed his eyes, instinctively drawing back against Max's hold. Max reinforced his grip on him and pressed the liquid into him. "James, you have to help. I don't want to force it down, but I will."

James swallowed several times. Choking, he pulled away strongly, until he broke Max's hold. "Max," he gasped, "I think I'd like to try it your way."

"Good boy." Max withdrew the cup slowly, releasing his trembling figure. "You waited long enough to change your mind."

"I think I drank some of it."

"You did. But I don't think enough to kill you."

"What is wrong with you, Max? Make him drink it all."

"James has changed his mind. He's decided to join us. We'll have to wait until Simeon returns. We'll let Pilchard decide what is to be done."

"It's too late. I've already decided. He can die this way, or he can die another way, but I want him dead."

"Shut up, Bandore. You're beginning to irritate me. James can be invaluable to Pilchard as his ally. If James says he is willing to help us, we need to let Pilchard decide whether or not he wants his help. All you have to do is keep your bloodthirsty instincts to yourself for a few days. If I'm wrong, you'll get to take care of James any way you want."

"And I'll get to take care of you, too." Bandore pointed a finger into Max's chest.

"I doubt you'll ever see that wish fulfilled, Bandore. If Simeon..."

"Max, I feel sick." James drenched in sweat thrashed in acute pain.

"I'm sorry, James. I'm afraid it can't be helped. Bandore, get the kit from my workroom. I'll see what I can do to make him comfortable through this."

Max stayed with James nursing him through each convulsive episode. As each fit of wrenching passed, James breathlessly whispered to Max, "I think that's it. I feel much better." He again doubled over in agony.

When the last of his writhing subsided, Max admonished him. "That was a very foolish thing to do. But perhaps it will work out better this way. Bandore's testimony will mean a lot with Pilchard, and now Bandore's convinced you're afraid to die."

"I am afraid to die."

"Yes, but not as much as you believe. It was foolish to swallow the poison."

"I couldn't help it. You were pushing it down my throat."

"Yes, I was," Max chuckled at his agitation. "But you knew I would be." He glanced at him with a glint in his eye. "Unfortunately around here I have more opportunity to mix poison than to heal the sick or wounded. Usually, I mix, and Bandore hurries away with it to give it to some poor soul he's marked as prey. This is the first time, to my recollection, that I've actually given it. I can't say I enjoyed it. But, if you hadn't changed your mind, I would have made you drink it —every last drop. I would have considered it a mercy killing." Max burst into laughter at his thoughts. "What a thought, my mercy or Bandore's! That isn't much of a choice. Oh, James, lighten up. You are alive, and I intend to keep you that way. At least, I'll try to. Although, I really don't know why."

24

The wind from the lake caressed Erin's face, a ghostly reminder of James's visit. She leaned against the balcony railing. Her heart agonized, the thought of losing him threading confusion through her mind. Through her tears, she watched the brilliant patterns from the Jewel of Light churning against the crisp sky. As she watched, peace spread within her carrying in its wake a steeled determination. She hurried into the suite. Inside her bedroom, she shoved a few personal items into a knapsack. As she finished packing the bag, her sister entered the room.

"Where are you going?" Janus followed her sister's movements with concern.

"I'm riding to the Arca V'ing Enta." Erin grabbed her bag and ran out of the suite and down the stairway. Janus followed her across the lawns to the stables. When she caught up with her, Erin was preparing a horse to ride.

"Will you wait?" In frustration, Janus pulled Erin towards her. "Why are you going to the Arca V'ing Enta? It's late."

"I don't have time to explain." Erin tore herself from Janus' grasp.

Janus called a stable attendant and, with his help, quickly prepared a mount.

"What are you doing?" Erin retorted.

"I'm going with you. You can't ride to the Arca V'ing Enta alone."

"You can't come with me." Erin mounted, prodding her horse into a run.

"Yes, I can." Janus mounted her horse in defiance. Soon, she was keeping pace with her sister. They rode silent and swift until the brilliant structure of the Arca V'ing Enta loomed ahead of them along the horizon. At its sight, Janus drew in a quick breath in amazement.

"It's beautiful, isn't it?" Erin said in awe as they reared their horses along the lake to rest.

"It's so pretty, it's scary." Janus started to climb down from her horse.

"I'm not staying here. I've got to get alongside it," Erin warned her sister. She guided her horse to the Arca V'ing Enta, walking along its edge.

"What are you looking for?" Janus called with impatience.

"I'm looking for a place to go through."

"You can't go through the Arca V'ing Enta!"

"Oh, yes, I can." She dismounted. Holding the reins in her hands, she walked along the arc. "Janus, will you take care of my horse?"

Janus slid off her mount. "What am I supposed to do with it?"

"I don't know. Wait for a while. If I'm not back soon, take it back to the stables."

"You're serious about this." In disbelieve, Janus took the reins from Erin. "You're actually going to try to go through that thing." Before she could stop her, Erin propelled herself into the colors of the Arca V'ing Enta and disappeared.

Erin fell to her hands and knees, her eyes blinded by the light filling the inside sanctuary of the Arca V'ing Enta. As she tried to adjust to the unsettling environment, she realized she could not sense direction, neither up nor down, and felt suspended in the warmth of a friendly womb. She tried to move, but couldn't. Time stilled. She waited, until her eyes caught sight of a spark of light fluttering within the brilliant glow. As her gaze locked to the sparkling light, she was freed from restraint. With joy, she followed the darted movements of the light with graceful fluidity, running and turning in rhythm, her dance to the elusive light. The light spun her around and around and around, until an unknown force lifted her with speed through the colors of the Arca V'ing Enta.

Erin fell to the ground stunned. As her head cleared, she heard excited chatter approaching her. A familiar voice suddenly rang out, "Erin! Benjamine, it is Erin!"

She looked up to the Artist bending over, his face exuberant in welcome. Benjamine peered from behind his back. "Don't be afraid now, Benjamine. It's only our Erin," the Artist consoled. "Benjamine came rushing at me, scared to death, interrupting my work. He was yelping that he saw a woman come through the Arca V'ing Enta. 'Impossible,' I said. But look at you. Here you are in flesh and blood."

"He can see me now?" Erin filled with excited surprise.

"He most certainly can." The Artist extended a hand to assist her in rising. Erin solidly clasped his hand as she rose, feeling the presence of flesh upon flesh.

"I made it." Erin hugged the Artist in relief.

"Yes, you did. But that was a dangerous stunt."

"I had to come through. James is in trouble."

"James?" The Artist ventured, his eyes twinkling.

"Yes, James. The man we saw at the Eastereven Ball. I've met him again. Pilchard's men are going to kill him."

"Pilchard, oh, dear." The Artist shook his head, dread crossing his face. In sympathy, he took Erin by the hand. "Pilchard is a dangerous man. His men, I'm afraid, may have already…"

"No, he's still alive. I feel it. I would feel it if something happened to him."

The Artist brushed her hand against his cheek as he bowed in respect. "You must love him very much."

"I do. He's a part of me, very deep within the heart of my spirit. I can't let him die." Urgency filled Erin's eyes.

The Artist looked over at Benjamine. "Benjamine, when you were in the village last, any word about Sir James?"

"No, Sir. Only some talk he never showed for the concert here. The others came, but he wasn't with them."

"They came without him? Oh, this doesn't look good. Well, we won't worry about the small stuff. Better not to stuff our heads with details. We need to concentrate on our main objective. Benjamine, go to the Mayhew estate and tell Lord Mayhew I've reconsidered. I'll let him have the piece he likes for the price he mentioned plus two horses. Tell him I'll have the two horses and one third up front. The rest I'll take upon delivery of my work."

"Yes, Sir, but what if he thinks it's too much? The plus two horses, I mean."

"How could he think it's too much? My goodness, it's my work, Benjamine. Lord Mayhew knows how rare it is I sell my work. But, if he says it's too much, settle for the two horses. Tell him I want them today, and bring them back here right away." The Artist chased Benjamine to see him quickly on his way.

With Benjamine gone, the Artist and Erin went into the hut to make their plan. "It won't be easy to find him," the Artist expressed his concern. He smacked his hands together. "We'll have to be systematic. We must start at Yves."

"I'm sure he's not at Yves," Erin contradicted him. "He was traveling, performing at different places along the way. He spoke with me every night."

"You spoke with him? Huh. Imagine that. Did he say where he was?"

"No, but I'm sure I can find him." Erin touched the crystal wing lying on her bosom under her clothing.

"Well, then we can assume he was with his musical company, but he never reached Eastereven. He was captured by Pilchard somewhere between Yves and Eastereven. There is a long distance between the two." The Artist drummed his fingers in consternation against his thigh.

Erin groped with her memory. "I remember when I spoke with him, he was in a place called, I think, Alton. Yes, I think that's what he called it. Then I didn't hear from him for a long time. When I did, he said they were going to kill him."

"Alton. I think I know where that is. It's still a long ways from here."

"I know wherever he is it's closed in, dark and very damp. I can feel it even now." Erin shuddered.

"You've described every root cellar, dungeon and prison in Fiara, I'm afraid. Don't worry. Alton will be a good place to start." The Artist petted her hand.

"If you lend me a horse, I'll just ride. I'll know where to find him." She was interrupted by the sound of horses breaking terrain near the hut.

They left the hut meeting Benjamine as he tethered the horses. The Artist called out to him in haste, "Good work. Now help me fill the bags with supplies so we can be on our way. We mustn't waste time."

Benjamine hurried preparing the horses. While they filled the bags, the Artist asked for the advance he had requested from Mayhew.

"I don't have it, Sir," Benjamine apologized. "I told Lord Mayhew you would be by to pick it up yourself."

"Myself. Benjamine, we haven't the time. I asked you to carry it here."

"Yes, Sir, I know, but I thought it would give you good reason to visit Lord Mayhew today. You see, I discovered Sir John never returned to Yves. He's been staying with Mayhew since the concert. I thought you would want the opportunity to speak with him."

"He's there now?" The Artist touched Benjamine's shoulder for assurance.

"Oh yes, Sir. He's resting in the guest parlor to the left of the back stairwell. The servants assured me he wouldn't be going anywhere for the rest of the day."

"Benjamine, you truly have a gift," the Artist commended him with glee. "Erin," he handed her the reins for one of the horses. "We'll ride to Mayhew's first. It may save us some time with our search. Benjamine, my good friend, tell no one where I've gone, and don't speak a word to anyone about Erin. For goodness sake, someone might actually believe you, and we mustn't have that." The Artist struggled mounting his own horse. With vehemence, he heeled the horse into a run. Benjamine sadly watched him ride away. Loneliness gripped him, as Erin and his friend were swallowed by the green thickness of the Eastereven forest.

The boisterous voice of the Artist drifted down the hall as he argued with Mayhew. Erin knocked several times on the hard wood of the heavy door blocking her entrance to the guest parlor. When no one answered, she tried opening it. She crept quietly into the antiquated splendor of the room. Erin's eyes scanned the room, resting on a man lying in a stupor on the parlor floor. She went to him and gently prodded his shoulder to arouse him. At her touch, he swatted the air in anger and curled himself to avoid disruption.

With patience, Erin touched his shoulders again and again, shaking him into awareness. "Excuse me. If you are John, I need to talk with you."

With her insistence, John uncurled himself. Erin helped him to a sitting position. As he leaned his back against the sofa, his sight cleared. Erin's dainty figure came into view.

"I need to talk with you." Erin repeated as his unfocused stare broke.

"I don't want to be disturbed."

"I need to talk with you now," Erin persisted.

"And who are you?" John rested his forehead in the palm of his hands.

"I'm a friend of James."

John's body tightened. He removed his hands to get a better view of her.

"I don't remember you," he said warily searching her face without recollection.

"You wouldn't. I don't know you, but James and I are very close."

"Oh, you are? It seems I would know you then." John eyed her with suspicion.

"I haven't time to explain everything, but I know something has happened to James. I know Pilchard's men are going to hurt him, and I have to find him before they do."

John's pale complexion reddened. "I don't know where you got your information, but you're mistaken."

"Then where is he?" Erin's words exploded.

"How should I know? We were resting in Alton, and he got up in the middle of the night and left. He got sick of it all and just left in the middle of a tour."

"That's not true," Erin protested.

"I was there. You weren't."

Erin turned from him, frustrated. "It doesn't matter. I was hoping you would help me, but I'll find him myself."

"You won't find him," he blurted out in a quiet voice cracking with emotion. He avoided the pained look she returned him.

"I'll find him." She started for the door.

"Not where they've taken him." John jutted his chin, his fear fighting against his compassion.

"You know where he is then." Erin felt pinched as she waited.

John's head throbbed. He dropped his gaze to the floor. "I couldn't do anything about it," he defended himself. "They came to me and said they had him. I was to send a message to Caldwell. I did. 'James has deserted us. I will go on alone.' I will go on alone. How brave of me, eh? I didn't know what to do, so I did as they asked. I still don't know what to do about it." He dropped his head in shame. The silence of the room seemed to swirl before he looked back up at her. "They've taken him to Pilchard. You'll never find your way in there. It's a natural fortress."

"I'll have to try."

"Then I better go with you. I'm the only one who has a chance of getting inside."

25

Simeon Pilchard watched the candle drip until only a puddle of wet tallow remained engulfing the flame. He sat brooding as its last flicker lit the night air. By the time he climbed down the mountain and made his way back through the Epping Wall, his men would have infiltrated many of the towns and villages across Fiara and his market for Grogg would be firmly established within the general populace over the next few months. From then, it would only be a matter of time before Simeon gathered the support he needed to control the noblemen at court and, eventually, the Queen. It had always been his plan, since the day she first shunned him for the Lord of Ashby-Oane.

Simeon knew he would succeed. He could feel it. A dark, strong cloud of force gathered like a sturdy vise within him. Perhaps, the lords in the west would muster a resistance against his reign, but there were few who could stop him now. Lord Eastham and his men were only a dressing Pilchard stealthily used to distract the Queen. Lord Eastham kept his men at bay along the Epping Wall to give the Queen a sense of security. Simeon wanted the Queen to feel secure, until the very last moment. The men Lord Eastham killed or captured were expendable. They helped give her that security. As for Lord Eastham, when the time was right, Pilchard knew he would bring him into tow through the habit of his daughter. He had already laid the groundwork. No. He worried about no one, except the bearer of the crystal wing. The Seer had warned him. He knew he must take it for his own.

The wind billowed and shuddered against the walls of the hut, threatening to tear it down, piece by piece. It carried the frantic sobs and helpless whimpering of the Seer within its gusts. Her moaning cry was swallowed and belched within the rolling flailing of the wind. Simeon looked up and gruffly snorted with disgust. He had first heard of the Seer from the storyteller who chanted of the crystal wing. In all of Fiara, only the Seer could help him find it. Simeon had boldly ridden to the high cliffs along the sea leading to her mountain lair. Climbing the fearsome rocks that guarded her hiding place, Simeon found her sitting in front of her hut at the peak of the treacherous slopes of the mountain. At first, he tried to befriend her, but when she resisted, a terrible anger stirred within him. It took time for Simeon to loosen her tongue. Like a furious storm, he ripped her stubborn silence, shred by shred. In the end, she was helpful.

She had a gift, she told him, a gift of dreams. Sometimes, answers to questions came to her while she slept. She knew about the crystal wing and had seen it in her dreams. Through torturous duress, Simeon enlisted her gift for his search. It would take time, she appealed to him, frightened by his brutality. There were no guarantees.

With the help of the Seer, Simeon's men tracked the old man across Fiara. Her clear visions brought them closer and closer to success. Many times, the old man barely slipped through their clutches. He was elusive. The people, closed mouth. One day, the old man disappeared, leaving only a cloud of mystery for Simeon to fathom. The mystery didn't daunt Simeon. He returned to the Seer.

The Seer swore to Simeon that she did not know where the old man had gone. After rigorous testing, Simeon spared her. She had useful skills, and he needed her help to complete his plans. With her vision, Simeon sculpted a design to overthrow the Queen. Working on the plan appeased his violent outbursts against the Seer, who continued to swear that her dreams revealed nothing of the old man or his magical wing.

It took years of consultation with the Seer before the plan was ready to coordinate. Bandore became instrumental in developing support from within the royal court. He implemented an outline for power through manipulation, fear and coercion within the ranks of the nobility itself. Bandore secured new followers by secretly supplying them with a personal supply of Grogg. The brew, along with his heinous acts of terror, encouraged an army bonded to Pilchard to form within the castle walls. Once Bandore managed to elicit the assistance of the more prominent members of the Royal Order of Musicians, the plan unfolded rapidly. When Bandore sent Pilchard word that James and John had begun their broad tour of Fiara, Simeon prepared to leave for another visit to the Seer. It was crucial he find the bearer of the crystal wing before he could interfere with his plan.

As the Seer watched Simeon climb the dangerous cliffs to her dwelling, she knew it was useless to try to distract him. She could no longer keep it a secret. Her dreams had forewarned her.

"The old man is dead," she revealed without pressure from him when he arrived on the bluff overlooking the deep cavities of the mountain range. "Where the crystal wing is, I cannot tell."

Simeon refused to be deterred. "Then find out," he demanded. He waited for weeks at the mountain dwelling while the Seer meditated. When she produced no results, he threatened her.

"I've done all I can. If I haven't seen it yet, I may never see where it is."

Pilchard pulled her to her feet by her hair. "I've heard this for years. I'm tired of it."

Using her hair as a leash, he pulled her toward the hut. Grabbing a coil of rope from the outside wall of the hut, he bound her tightly. He dragged her toward the ledge, scraping her across the rocky ground. She quivered at the edge of the cliff as he repeatedly dangled her, taunting her with its drop. When she remained silent, he found more rope and lashed her against the jagged rock abutment along the ledge. It only took a short time before she broke with his questioning. In between her tears and gasping breath, she finally told him. She did not know where the crystal wing was, but she knew who had been with the old man when he died.

Pilchard spit on her. Leaving her bound helpless on the rocky ledge, he started for the cliff to begin his climb down the mountain. The wind stirred and gathered into a strong gale before he could find his first foothold. It blustered against him almost knocking him over the edge. Pulling himself back onto the ledge, he fought his way through the storm back into the hut, struggling to latch the door. He cussed, lit a candle, and sat down to wait out the storm.

The storm rattled the hut as it tore into frenzy. The ground rumbled. The shrieks of the Seer blended into the howling wind. Pilchard smiled. He lit another candle. When the weather broke, he could make his way down the mountainside back to his fortress. There he would arrange to take Sir James McCautry into his custody.

26

When they reached the border of the Epping Wall in Eastham, John gave his mount to Erin. He would try to cross the border into Pilchard alone. Erin's horse fought her as she took the reins to John's mount into her hands. As her horse reared, she warned John, "Get out any way you can. I'll find you."

John watched Erin and the Artist ride away, their dust kicking the air. Unexpectedly, Erin pulled her horse around and rode back toward John. Reaching him, she walked the horse alongside him.

"Tell James to wear it," she directed without further explanation, and then rode to rejoin the Artist.

Wondering about Erin's words, John made his way on foot along the rocky terrain leading to the Epping Pass. He saw the smoke from the campfires of Lord Eastham's men dotting the landscape beyond him. As he approached the pass, he took shelter behind a rock abutment along the base of the wall. There, he waited for dusk to wane into darkness before attempting to move through the military line guarding the entrance to Pilchard.

When night overcame the land, John crawled along the base of the Epping Wall, his figure concealed by its deep shadows and overpowering structure. As he moved into the narrow pass, his nerves tightened, preparing for the reception he knew waited at its end. He crept onto the desolate mountain land beyond the pass and was overrun by Pilchard's watchmen. While John argued, asking to see Bandore, the men bound and blindfolded him. After gagging him, they forced him in haste along a steep and rocky path. The path was difficult for John to tread. In spite of their strong hold on him, he stumbled and fell. They pushed him to keep him moving through the upward climb. The long walk was broken when they tugged him into a sitting position onto the ground. Feigning confidence, he waited for their next move, his nostrils flaring with the chill of the night air. He heard the shuffling of feet and shifting bodies near him. An occasional cough exploded into the night, ravaging his unsteady calm.

The blind vigil ended with the tight grip of hands pulling him to his feet and roughly guiding him forward. Their footsteps sounded fuller. A slight echo tinged the air. John smelled mustiness, and dampness played along his skin, cooling him. A firmer grip squeezed him. Hands clasped his legs. Someone lashed his legs together. Stone scraped along his body as he felt a push. He fell through the air, soon connecting with hard rock of solid ground. Stunned, he vaguely heard the sound of footsteps fading above him. He lay still, until footsteps again disrupted the deep silence and a voice cackled above his head.

"What are you doing here, John?"

John breathed deeply waiting for Bandore's voice to break the quiet again. He heard the sound of departing footsteps badger the air. John lay in the contained darkness, his discomfort threatening to overcome him. Once again, he heard the sound of approaching footsteps. Someone entered the space and removed his bonds. Using a rope, the men pulled John through the opening overhead. They escorted him through narrow tunnels to Bandore's quarters.

"You came looking for James," Bandore greeted him with displeasure. He walked back and forth in front of John. "It's a stupid thing to do."

"I was hoping to work something out with you. You haven't killed him?"

"Not yet. His execution has been postponed." Bandore stopped pacing. He pointed his chin towards John. "We have a difference of opinion here. Pilchard will settle it as soon as he returns."

"You have a difference of opinion?"

"Max thinks James could be useful to us." Bandore puckered his upper lip in a scowl.

"You think he's wrong."

"James won't go through with it. You know that. Sooner or later we'll have to get rid of him. It's better to do it now."

A burning sensation flooded John's neck and spread along the sides of his face into his cheekbones. "I understand your point, but he's still my friend. If there is another way, I'd like you to consider it."

Bandore smiled. "Your tour went well in spite of the trouble. I was told we accomplished more than we hoped for. You were smart to keep going."

"I did what I was told."

"Yes. Yes, you did. And that's what we need. You want to see James? I'll arrange that for you. But it might be easier for you if you went home now."

"No, I want to see him," John stayed his ground.

Bandore stared at him, scrutinizing his motives. "Where we've detained him the tunnels are even more of a maze than in here. They go for great distances, but they lead nowhere. They're all dead ends. Keep it in mind. He'll stand a better chance with Pilchard."

"All right, Bandore. I hear you." John looked at the ground.

Bandore laughed. He took John by the arm leading him out of his quarters into an adjacent tunnel. There, he instructed a guard to escort John through the tunnels to James.

At the sound of someone approaching, Max went outside the cell entrance. James heard a hushed muttering from the dark shadows outside. When James realized that the man following Max back into the cell was John, his hope fanned. As he looked into John's eyes, the hope igniting in him transformed into concern. His gaze went from Max to John. Resting on John, his eyes filled with sadness and mirrored the questions plaguing him.

The look in James's eyes pulled the smile from John's lips. "Yes, I'm involved with them," John admitted with shame. "That's got nothing to do with you. You're still my friend. I've asked Bandore to take that into consideration."

James moved to thank him, but could not find words. Feeling deserted, he leaned his back against the cold rock wall. A tear escaped the corner of his eye. Max noting the wet streak rolling down the side of James's face turned to John in compassion. "I can give you a little time alone, if you'd like."

James wiped his face with the palm of his hand. "I'm all right, Max. You don't have to leave."

Without regarding James's words, Max took a torch from the wall and left. John waited until the sound of Max's footsteps were distant. When he spoke, he dropped the tone of his voice preventing the guards from hearing him.

"I've come to get you out of here, but I'm not sure if it's possible. I don't know the way in, so I'm not sure I can find the way out. I promised your friend, Erin, I would get you out any way I could. I don't think she understands the danger. She doesn't see how impossible it will be to come out of this at all, let alone out of it and be the same."

"You spoke with Erin?" James's heart beat rapid at the thought.

"She's waiting for us somewhere outside the pass."

"She's here in Fiara?"

"Where else would she be?" John asked confused.

"I don't believe this. This is great!" James threw his arms around his friend in joy.

"All right, keep it down." John quieted him. "If it means anything to you, she said to tell you to wear it. What is 'it'?"

James motioned John for secrecy. With John guarding his action, he went to the rock ledge and ran his fingers along the wall. He dislodged the rock encasing the crystal wing. After wiping the wing clean with a corner of his shirt, he held it up for John to see. James hushed his surprised look and placed the crystal wing around his neck, letting it hang underneath his shirt.

"I think I can take that guard," John muttered to him. "But I'm not sure what to do then. What do you think? Should we wait? Maybe I can talk us out of here."

"No, I want to be out of here before Pilchard returns." James grasped the crystal wing under his shirt.

"And how are we going to do that?"

"She said any way we can."

"Yes, but..."

A noise in the tunnel interrupted them. Max came to the cell entrance. "I can only give you a few more minutes. A watchman has informed me Pilchard is back. I expect Bandore will be sending for James soon. I'm going to my workroom to pick up a few items I might need. The guards will take you both there in a few minutes. It's on the way. You understand. I can't give you more time than that."

They waited until Max was well out of range. When a guard entered to bind James, John crushed him against the rock wall with a chair. "Get out of here now," he called to James.

James advanced to assist him. As he did, the guard freed himself from John. Knocking John to the ground, the guard met James head-on, grappling him. John quickly got to his feet. Grasping the fallen chair, John struck the guard along his back bringing him to the floor.

"Let's get out of here." John pulled James to his feet.

"Is he all right?"

"We haven't time for that." John tugged at him to run. When they reached the tunnel outside the door, they both hesitated.

"Which way do we go?" John, looking down the tunnel, saw a light moving toward them, warning them of more guards.

"Let's try this way." James grabbed a torch from the wall. They chose a tight passageway, the only free route for escape.

"Bandore said these tunnels lead nowhere," John warned him with growing nervousness.

"And you believe Bandore?"

"It's a fair bet he's right."

The sound of the guards fast on their trail grew louder, pushing them to hasten their steps. When they reached bisecting tunnels, they paused confused.

"I can find the way," James convinced himself out loud.

"How can you do that? Come on. Let's go this way." John pulled at him with mounting fear.

"No. Not that way." James stood still. He searched the area with his eyes, trying to sense direction.

"We don't have time to be picky, James. Come on."

"No. I can find it. I know I can find it."

"Find what? Can't you hear? They're coming."

James moved into one of the tunnels, running the torch close to the wall to see clearer. "It's here, John," he called to him. He handed him the torch, pointing to a small opening high in the side of the wall.

"We're not going in there."

"This is the way. I'm sure of it," James reassured him. "I'll go first. Put the torch out before you come through."

"It doesn't look big enough to get through," John remarked.

"It's plenty big enough," James said as he found a foothold in the wall. He lifted himself and wriggled through the opening.

John secured a hold on the opening before extinguishing the torch, enclosing them in blackness. Fighting an upsurge of panic, he pushed the torch into the crawl space ahead of him. Even in the darkness, he sensed the minimal clearance provided by the crawl space. As they moved through the space, the muffled sounds of the guards passing by the opening reached them and dissolved into silence.

"They're gone," John dared speak. "Shouldn't we go back?"

"No. Keep going."

"Keep going! I can't see anything. I'm not even sure where you are."

"I'm ahead of you. Just keep going," James instructed.

"Keep going? It's hard to breathe in here."

"Keep going anyway." With determination, James moved ahead through the darkness. They crawled for what seemed an endless amount of time before James gave into his fatigue and lay face down in the crawl space.

"I'm sorry, John. I've got to rest."

"It's about time," John grumbled from behind him.

"We should have thought to bring some water. I could use some now," James moaned.

John broke into laughter. "I don't think that would really make a difference at this point."

They settled into silence, drifting into uncomfortable sleep. Finally, James forced himself to move forward, calling John to follow him. As they crept through the cramped blackness, John despaired, "This never ends. We've come the wrong way."

"No, I'm sure this is the way."

They rested several times before the crawl space emptied into a larger compartment. James dragged himself to his knees, feeling his surroundings with his hands. He was pushed to the ground as John leaned into him from within the darkness. After disentangling themselves, they ran their hands along the compartment walls trying to find an exit.

"There's enough air," James quipped defensively.

John sat down in resignation. "We're trapped. We better go back."

"No. I know this is right. I can feel it."

"There is nothing here, James. There's no way out."

"You don't understand. I can feel it," James argued.

"Feel what? There is nothing here. It's a dead-end, just as Bandore said."

Holding the crystal wing in one hand, James ignored John's words. He ran his other hand along the compartment wall again. "Here," he cried out loud with discovery and began digging furiously with his hands.

"What are you doing?" John questioned from the darkness.

"Help me dig."

"Help me dig. You're digging? Are you crazy?" John moved closer to James as he dug into the wall in panic. "You're bringing the wall down on us."

"No. No, I'm not. Help me dig. It's hard going here. Use the torch handle."

John hit the torch handle into James's hand. James took the handle when he felt it touch his hand. He used it to scrape past the first layer of hard dirt. As the dirt softened beneath his fingers, James handed the torch handle back to John. With frantic movement, he dug with both hands. In the darkness, he felt John's hands moving in the dirt. A soft stream of light suddenly penetrated the darkness of the compartment. James felt the touch of another hand through the dirt. He dug faster until a larger opening broke the wall, and hands dragged him through the dirt and grime into the light of dawn. He fell into Erin's warm embrace and clung to her in desperate passion as the Artist helped John to the surface.

"Imagine that," the Artist mused examining the hole in the side of the hill. "She really could find him."

"That's great, but we're not safe yet," John reminded him with a hint of sarcasm. "We've got to get out of here before Pilchard finds where we've gone."

"Let's go then." The Artist slipped down the embankment to the horses. He mounted his own horse and led the others to the hillside for his companions. "James, you'll have to ride with Erin," the Artist called to him. He handed James the reins. "She found the way here; she'll have to find the way back for us. We came through the bogs."

"The bogs," John yelped. "Then we're still in Pilchard."

"Technically, that's probably so." The Artist scratched his head. "I'd say we are just beyond the bogs, but we're not far from Fiara. It didn't seem to take us very long to get here."

"But how could you come through the bogs?" John asked him as he mounted his horse.

"I followed Erin, of course."

"Of course," John echoed with cynicism. He grabbed the edge of the rope James offered him and spurred his horse into movement.

As they made their way down the rocky slopes of the mountain, the thick fog skirting the marshlands swallowed them. Erin and James led the way through the wet mire. The rope they held between the horses kept them together in the murky swirl of the bogs. When the fog thinned and the land stiffened under the horses' hooves, John dropped the rope and rode alongside James and Erin, urging them to a halt.

"I think we should ride to Lord Eastham's from here. It's closer than Yves, and he can fend off Pilchard for us."

"You're probably right," James sighed. He held Erin closer.

"James," Erin wrapped her hands tenderly in his as she spoke. "I have to bring the crystal wings back."

James pressed his forehead against the top of her head in distress. He tucked her even closer into his body. "I'm taking you home with me," he whispered in earnest.

"I have to take them back. It's too dangerous for both crystal wings to be here."

"I'm going with you. Can you handle it alone?" He asked John, pleading.

"Alone against Pilchard and Bandore," the Artist admonished him with frank boldness.

"Bandore is sure to set me up after this. With you gone, it will be easy for him to do. The Queen will never believe me, if you disappear from Fiara."

"You better go back with John." Heaviness etched its way through Erin's heart. "I can ride with the Artist back to Eastereven."

"No. I'll take you there." James felt scalded. "John, you can ride with me or I can meet you back at Yves."

"I'll go with you."

James brushed his lips along Erin's cheeks, and then jostled his horse into a gallop. They rode through the countryside taking infrequent rests. James kept Erin close to him. "I'm losing a part of myself," he thought. He dreaded every mile bringing them closer to Eastereven and the Arca V'ing Enta.

When the Artist spotted the Arca V'ing Enta bridging the sky ahead of them, he announced, "We're almost there."

With the Artist's words, an ache swelled within James. His hope dissipated with the light from the Arc emanating along the horizon. James resisted an impulse to pull his horse around and head into the wilds of Fiara with Erin. Instead, he tightened his grasp around her and moved his steed forward.

When they reached the Arca V'ing Enta, James helped Erin dismount. As they walked along the Arc's edge, James removed the crystal wing from his neck and placed it over Erin's head. He took her into his arms. "I'll always love you," he whispered in her ear. He turned to leave her. Erin broke into tears.

"I can't let you go," She reached out to touch him. As James turned, trying once again to connect with her warmth, the Artist pushed her backward into the energy of the Arca V'ing Enta.

"No!" James cried out. His voice echoed and dissolved as Erin's figure faded out of sight.

"Why did you do that?" James screamed at the Artist. He shook him fiercely in anger, his own body quaking.

"Somebody had to," the Artist sadly replied.

Trembling, James released the Artist. He felt John's strong hands take hold of him. "Come on," John sternly said knowing he was unable to bring him comfort. "We have to get back to Yves."

James, numb and pale, mounted his horse and rode away from the light of the Arca V'ing Enta, across the countryside toward the castle Yves.

THE CRYSTAL WINGS

27

Erin picked herself up from the grass. Confused, her eyes searched the countryside looking for James. Her tears burned her as she wandered along the Arca V'ing Enta caressing the crystal wings with her hands. Her soul yearned for James, a vise draining her of purpose. "I can go back," she thought. "I have both wings now."

Without aim, she moved toward the light bordering the edge of the Arca V'ing Enta, drawn to James and the world hidden beyond its light. As she did, she sensed a higher purpose and forced herself to walk away from the Arca V'ing Enta. The sound of horses rumbled through her head as she moved further and further away from the magnificent arc.

"Where have you been?" Her sister climbed from her mount and threw her arms around her. "I've been back every day since you left. Hoping I'd see you. Hoping you'd come home."

Erin openly sobbed in her sister's embrace. Through her tears, she noticed her horse. "You brought me something to ride."

"Every day I rode here with your horse, praying you'd come home. Everyone is so worried about you."

"You didn't tell them, did you?"

"I haven't told a soul."

Erin wiped her eyes and brought herself under control. "Janus, I've one thing left to do. Trust me one more time. Leave me the horse and go back to the university alone."

"Erin."

"Come on, Janus. Please, do as I ask."

Janus reluctantly handed the reins for the horse to Erin. She went to her own horse and mounted. "You better not try to go through that thing again," she cautioned her sister before riding away.

Erin wanted, more than anything else, to ride the horse through the Arca V'ing Enta and return to the one she loved. Instead, she rode to the mountain holding the Jewel of Light. At the bottom of its slopes, she tied her horse and walked through the forest to the wall blocking the way to the Jewel. As she reached the wall, Erin felt a surge of energy from the power of the crystal wings. She lightly touched the surface of the wall with both hands. All along its vast structure, the wall quaked and shivered until, with an echoing roar, it crumbled before her. She walked over the rubble and began to weep, realizing she could do anything with the power of the crystal wings.

Making her way to the base of the Jewel of Light, she knelt and removed the wings from their chains. One at a time, Erin placed the crystal wings into their settings. When the last crystal wing settled into place, a light burst from the Jewel of Light with the force of an explosion, throwing Erin to the ground and blinding her. When her sight finally cleared, she saw that the crystal wings had mended, and were hovering in the air, sparkling and brilliant. She reached out to touch them, but her hand passed through them. Over and over again, her hands passed through them. She covered her face, got to her feet and stumbled across the meadow away from the Jewel. The thought of her beloved James ripped through her soul. It burned her until she found it painful to draw in a breath. She turned to look at the Jewel one more time. Through her tears, she watched the shimmering glow from within the Jewel expand and rise into the night. It moved across the dark sky and fell like a blanket of pure light upon the sleeping city of Esaunum below.

"...then they shall find peace and love, when two worlds become one."

The Legend of Justlevenoma

Acknowledgements

I would like to thank Mathew Chiuchiolo, Dolores Fontana, Missy Haber, Darcy Engle and Jan Fortier for reading the story and encouraging me to publish it; my mother and father for gently spurring me to be true to my artistic self; Amanda Fortier for the time she spent helping me to edit the book for publication; Jean Watson, my friend and teacher; Alyson Boudreault, Scott Beck, Susanna Walden and the many people who have had a part in the publication of *The Crystal Wing*.

www.ingramcontent.com/pod-product-compliance
Lightning Source LLC
Chambersburg PA
CBHW060906250626
47159CB00008B/2888